BEFORE THE RAIN

BEFORE THE RAIN

A PANEGYRIC

W. PENKETHMAN-CARR

Troubador Publishing Ltd
Unit E2 Airfield Business Park,
Harrison Road, Market Harborough,
Leicestershire LE16 7UL
Tel: 0116 279 2299
Email: books@troubador.co.uk
Web: www.troubador.co.uk

ISBN 978 1 80514 479 3

British Library Cataloguing in Publication Data.
A catalogue record for this book is available from the British Library.

Typeset in 11pt Minion Pro by Troubador Publishing Ltd, Leicester, UK

To Kieran

"And what shall I love if not the enigma?"
– Giorgio de Chirico

I dreamt that I came to the edge of a vertiginous cliff, so tall that to look straight down would make you go mad. The cliffs did not face out to sea; below me, there lay a canyon and another set of cliffs faced me from the far side. On that other side, a city blended with the cliff. It appeared in a desert haze, partially obscured by dust and sand, making me think of Mexico City and Las Vegas – a cross between the imagination of J.G. Ballard and Max Ernst. The architecture was akin to the Nazi designs for Berlin, had they won the war. Leviathans, carved from the rock face, held themselves against the sky. The city was on four storeys, cradled within the canyon. Superhighways intersected at different levels. It felt like a lifetime would be too short to travel from one district to another.

And then, apropos of nothing, I was at a tower far away from the city. I sat in a circle around a fire with others who I did not recognise. Snow lightly drifted around us; we were warm in the orange glow. Then, we got the word: we could climb the great staircase and meet the unknown god. We suddenly jumped up and everyone was loaded with a rug on their shoulders – whether it was to keep us warm at the top or was part of some symbolic ritual, I was unsure.

We ran to the tower. It stood very tall, narrow, square and made entirely of polished wood. We raced up the wooden steps. I was second to last going up – the one behind me was an unknown companion whose identity was blurred. We continued racing up; I knew that if I lost sight of the guiding group going up, then they'd be forever lost to me. I somehow knew that if I did not keep up, then it was as good as not following at all – one cannot catch up. I knew this because I have had this dream before and I had been left behind. I refused to let this happen again, but my companion lagged. There were suddenly multiple rooms (as if the tower's interior had suddenly widened to accommodate them) and this person went into one of them (very dark – a place where someone slept) and got a further blanket. How I knew that this was what they were doing, I do not know, but I knew it with the strange certainty that is characteristic of dreams. Nor do I know the significance of the second blanket – I leave all that to the analysts.

I still had not quite lost sight of the rest of the group and as I reached the top, I saw the queue to the final trapdoor that led to the roof. I turned and called down to my companion, who was on the floor below, and received no response. When I turned back, the rest of them had gone. I left my companion without thinking – another lost soul whose importance to me I could never fathom. I rushed to the trapdoor and saw that it was barely big enough to put my hand in. I squeezed my hand through, nonetheless, and someone grabbed it, as if in solidarity, but perhaps it was to pull me to the otherside.

A voice called down to say that I had two messages from the god. The messages were two names, written on different slips of paper. The first answer, I was told, was a name from my past. It floated down like snow; I missed it and it continued to drift down the tower. I thought to pick it up again on the way back down. Then, the second piece of paper floated down – a name from my future – and this time I caught it. Except it wasn't a name; it was a text written as a stream of consciousness, as if what had been written down was merely what they had been speaking about at the time. I cannot recall the words, but I do remember that I felt the answers to be disappointing.

***

Lately, my thoughts before going to sleep blindly form images and narratives. I do not realise I've conjured them until, for some inexplicable reason, I do, as if someone had just politely reminded me that I was thinking or dreaming. That original dream – or thought – repeated itself over the following nights, with minor variations on the same theme. Sometimes I would be told to leave, banished by nameless accusations, and looks would pass back and forth as if everyone knew that everything was scripted and had gone differently before and would change again. I even tried to remember a map of where I went in the dream tower and recall the faces that I would potentially recognise someday.

***

I thought to find out whether there was someone in the city where I lived (which city? I forget the name now. It doesn't matter – they all look increasingly the same) to ask them to interpret my dreams and find out their meaning – if they had any meaning whatsoever. Finding nobody (aside from sad-looking psychics), I wondered whether anyone should regard my dreams as having any significance whatsoever. After a while, I no longer questioned these kinds of dreams and I grew used to them, thinking about them academically and eventually relaxing into them, realising that my unconscious had opened a new fold in my imagination. As if on cue, I began to take night walks frequently, thinking about the dreams and the people within them, and I would return late at night, still thinking. The dreams broadened to encompass further themes, sometimes extending to such a duration that the following morning I felt I could almost write a film script out of them.

And it was during those long nights where I was deliberately provoking everything that I noticed new things around me, as if the world was getting high, like a precursor to something everyone only half-knew was approaching. On these night walks, I would witness things, voyeuristically watching people fall about in the darkness. Sometimes, from a distance, I could see the isolated silhouettes of figures who walked with a secret intention or, turning a corner, there they were, astonishingly close to me, and I would realise I had run into my mirror image and would face others who were also there quite unaccountably and who remained silent. While I sought nothing, I eventually came to see myself as a self-styled detective, looking for clues in an age that had become desolate. Putting it that way, it seems juvenile, but at the time it became a deadly serious endeavour. A sad policeman, involuntarily fascinated by the actions of humanity he can only call criminal, without quite being able to justify why he thinks that way.

And so, I would meander the streets and enter the bars with their illicit booths and backyards where people groaned and took part in strange ceremonies that I could only guess at. I trespassed a lot and do not mind saying that I broke into many people's properties. I found the dogging spots around the city's edges, but never once did I involve myself. Looking back, I cannot understand why I did not – I regret missing that opportunity. On the calm nights, I found myself by the river and would admire, from the other side of the bank, the tall, satanic towers of glass that promised nothing but their victory and a thousand suicides. It should be made clear also that in no way did I go out of my way to find these things. At most, I would follow an odd-looking couple and see where they led me; often, I merely happened upon the scene…

***

One evening, I did not go down the path that I wanted to follow. Beginning my ascent up the hill towards the castle, I had been spotted: the tallest of a group of three men loitering outside a pub raised his arm and heckled at me to approach. As much as I immediately disliked them, I did not hesitate. The fact was that I was irrevocably caught, and I knew hesitation – the refusal to join the ritual – to be lethal around professional drinkers. Not being game was an automatic registration of distrust; a public avowal of separateness that cures itself only through provoking further jeers, which burn into the back of the head. Singled out among the crowd, I was uncomfortably sucked in by them and pulled into automatic obedience. With each step, I acknowledged their bizarre authority over me and I knew that I would have to go through with everything they wanted me to until they, at last, got bored. And yet, something about the sticky imposture revelled my mind: something was happening.

I approached, hoping to give nothing away. The man with the raised arm landed it around my shoulders, capturing me, and as he lathered my face with the warm guff of his breath, he said, apropos of nothing: 'Have you ever seen such a tiny penis?'. On cue, the shortest of the group stepped forward with a half-drunk pint in one hand and, with the other, unzipped his fly and presented me with his flaccid cock. I registered no surprise, nor did I recoil or look away. Used to not being spoken to, I was still thawing from being called upon. The penis was small, but my attention was oddly more drawn to the meticulously shaven crotch, so finely trimmed I wondered whether he had gone to the barbers to get it done.

'I'll be honest', I began, 'I don't see that many cocks out, so I don't have anything to compare it to.' I had hoped I had given a political answer, being at once true, inoffensive and non-committal. So far, I had only ever been a witness to things like this and wanted to retain my observer's stance. Besides, it also happened to be true that I had not often seen other men's penises, at least not since school and, even then, only inadvertently. (It has been a long time since I was an adolescent and felt insecure about whether it was normal.) I also did not want to offend the man with the small penis; caught in another man's grip, this guy could easily throw a punch and land it. It even occurred to me whether they were going to make me get my own penis out to compare them, but instead I was asked, 'Have you ever been to boarding school?'. I said I had not and they laughed.

The man with his cock out merely smiled at me and I realised that while I was examining this man's penis, he had been examining my face, pleasured for having his cock out, winning the bet another had presumably dared him to wager – an arrogant pride pulled off. I also noticed how his face was as well-shaven as his crotch – perhaps it had all been done at the same time – a full-body shave.

Then, the third man took a step back and said, as if to a crowd, 'He loves it – washes his mouth in come'; 'Bends over for all the boys'; 'Do you like it, eh? Is it good for you?'

I felt the arm release me in the laughter and I left, mutely offering goodnight to them, and disappeared back the way I had come, to be made into a story for them to tell others and then forgotten. I would replay this scene repeatedly as I walked on, nonplussed and annoyed that I had been disturbed. I could not understand why that was the thing they had chosen to do with their evening. It was sheer disruption; it shook me out of myself, making me do things as if I had been called upon. What is it that they *want*? What do they all want?

***

I felt I was amid chaos, intoxicated with an adulteration of the screen that separated the world and bodies from me.

I felt strange surges of knowledge that caused me to laugh behind my hand and gaze askance with looks of conspiracy at inanimate objects. That night of the first dream, I drafted what felt to me like a manifesto – an attempt to articulate this suspicion of the delirious autonomy of things going on behind everyone's backs, that things were not going to plan, that the machines were all breaking down, that things were coming to a close. I had a strong feeling that it was the end of things. For the world *was* ending, is still ending; it has always been ending, for, after all, that is what we have all been told by the rustle of waste in the gutter and the quietly apocalyptic speeches uttered by crying scientists. The project, however, did not survive beyond that first night. I think I still have those notes somewhere, but they must be buried somewhere deep.

***

There was something in the structure of the whole arrangement to the universe that I have always felt has kept me out of the picture; I was acknowledged, but it remained only at that. Nobody quite understood why I was there and, again, with hindsight, I suspect many of the clientele of bars, shops and cafés have felt uncomfortable seeing me there, apparently waiting for something. Soon, I also felt uncomfortable, being at once seen and immediately glossed over. I would ask myself why I had chosen this place specifically and as I repeatedly analysed it in my head, I would churn up answers that became more gross with each speculation.

I fled into other sides of the knotted city as it beckoned

my wandering gaze. I looked closer at things and people more so than I had ever done. For a long time, years, I had either stared straight ahead of me or down at the ground – I had missed so much. I went to strip joints, got to know some drug dealers and enjoyed getting high for the first time in my life. I took up a lively interest in cranes, industrial estates and the chatter in fast-food takeaways. On a hilltop with the city below me, I saw – with alien horror – a plateau of rooftops and cascading car parks set against the stars, which shone like eyes. I remembered as a child when I saw the stars reflected in a puddle, I would feel a sense of vertigo of potentially falling through this break in the universe – now, this vertigo extended before me as I stared at the night sky, and I wondered if everything I saw would suddenly start falling gelatinously upwards into the abyss. The way the streetlights burned in the distance told of an insecure anger that something else also thought this could come to pass and so stuck steadfastly to its welded iron, refusing the upwards pull. The sight was strangely silent; I had expected an omnipresent noise, but the silence was only broken by the occasional siren.

Filling the void was a dim hum, a feverish buzz that I thought would bring the onset of insomnia for the restless – a cursing call to permanent wakefulness. What was disquieting about this hum was that it was quiet enough for me to question whether it existed at all; it was as if it were inside the silence, or at least operating on an unknown plane. Like a bug, a helicopter might appear as if checking to see if everything were obediently still in place, then the hum would disappear temporarily and come out of hiding again once the scout had flown away. When I tried to write down this experience, I realised I sounded similar to some obscure conspiracy theorist for whom the demons existed only as strange noises and in the everyday things seen all the time but appearing nonetheless as monstrous.

***

During the day, I cross-referenced my nocturnal witnessing with what was on television. I amused myself with the prospect of watching a menagerie of various waning celebrities and politicians giving their views on the world to the general public and found that a distortion of what they said was followed by what I saw as a series of weird social meanderings. I wondered whether I should also follow their life advice, which encompassed any and all possible lives. It is difficult for me to put it the way I want to, but it was as if their principals were always already there. I then started rapidly changing the channels, never stopping for more than a few seconds each time. In bursts, I registered a mad amalgam of images and halted voices all in disjointed concert with each other. I wondered what happens when a life is made of this – what the inner eye sees. Human beings taken from birth to live on the outskirts of the continuous, incestuous reverberation of an infinity of programmes, and what happens when the electrified dreams of the average trigger-happy channel-flicker are eventually short-circuited by a grievous return to reality.

Halting the vicious panorama, I returned in more depth to the *personalities*. I especially liked their advice on war, which was eternally happening elsewhere, and their horror and sheer inability to conceive of morality's retreat by the onset of frozen pipes. Eventually, the fading figures gave way and devolved into talk-show hosts, and put their analyses into bite-size either/ors – are you for or against X? It occurred to me that people were spoiling for a war – a democratically elected one, perhaps via a referendum – with the celebrities in skin-tight clothes as generals slaughtering and sinking refugee boats. Swarmed by immigrants, as I was told this country was, the wars also had to be stopped to halt the immigrants and only then the supreme peace would presumably reign.

***

Outside, when it was night again, I could not but fail to glance at the groups in skin-tight dresses and oddly cut clothes to watch their strange gestures and theatrical performances. There was a desperation I saw to their carnival, something forced; nothing they wore looked comfortable nor anything they swallowed digestible. Plenty sat on the pavements, no longer caring how they looked, waiting for the alcohol to wear off and the taxi to arrive, stubbing out cigarette butts while someone tried to be funny. It was another culture I knew existed but hardly saw. Generally, I stayed away, unsure whether my brand of dissociative witnessing could be justified to anyone if I were caught and accused of voyeurism. (Why deny it, though? I am a voyeur. If I am ever arrested, I will not be able to argue myself out of that condemnation. Thus, I accept it. I accept I did something immoral and

I will smile at the policeman as he comes to arrest me.)

***

I once plucked a stranger's phone number out of the night air. I heard someone provide it to someone else just as they folded themselves into a taxi. By then, I had also recorded and called all the numbers I could find scrawled onto toilet walls by blocking my caller ID. I rang to find out who they were, inform them they were on the toilet walls and ask why they were there. Most of them never answered; other times, they immediately hung up, sometimes swearing at me. To those who never answered, I left messages.

***

I passed a street corner and saw that a fight had broken out. The crowd was apathetic, but the two combatants screamed at each other, seemingly over the contents of some takeaway box. The box was thrown into the gutter by the sweep of an arm; furious punches were thrown until one of them was on the floor. Some other passerby tried to quicken their step and leave the scene without interfering, but as I slowed down and stopped, so did they. It was as if I had unintentionally anchored them to the event alongside me. The crowd, including myself and the other person, stood and watched without intervening. The fighter, still standing, pulled the other to his feet, only to punch him again with finality, and the beaten one fell passively, already unconscious, his head landing on the curb's edge and echoing with a hollow crack. I felt that the other who had stopped alongside me hated me for making them bear witness to what we had just seen.

***

Met some weird folk. There was a homeless guy, who went by the name "Mushroom Ed" – nobody I spoke to knew exactly why he was called that. At a guess, it must have something to do with his disappearances and subsequent appearances around the city, growing like a mushroom spontaneously in the gaps on the street and in the parks. There was a tent on the side of the road, furniture, food, indecipherable pieces of paper, miscellaneous objects strewn about – if there are plastic bags contaminating the ocean floor, why not here?

I had not intended to stop when I once walked past, but he overtook and suddenly he stood in front of me. There was another man storming away from Mushroom Ed, who was shouting at strangers passing by while pointing in our direction. I found myself being spoken to by Mushroom Ed while the other unknown man continued to shout. He talked at me about how much he hated this place – whether he meant the local area, the city or the universe itself, I had no idea – and how two-faced and hypocritical people are, implying not just the person he had just fallen out with, but everyone, including me. I could not hear much of his murmuring voice and began to think on how I could politely leave, feeling eminently out-of-touch, wanting to flee in the face of this problematic person. I felt caught by the simple fact that I could easily do everything for Mushroom Ed, but when he asked if I could buy him a lamb curry – the specific dish done by a favourite Indian restaurant of his on the near side of town – I said no. Like everyone does, I made the excuse that I had to be somewhere – somewhere that demanded my presence – and that everything would presumably fall apart unless I appeared. The naked apparition of myself bled through my eyes and skin; nothing changed the fact that I preferred to keep my bank balance unmolested. In a later retroactive self-justification, I would half-heartedly argue that I still had not got used to involving myself; I still preferred myself as a spectator, even though that excused nothing and I knew it.

There were others who existed in a similar vein. There was one whom I dubbed "Virgil", given his unselfconscious pronouncements of apocalyptic politics that could sometimes be taken for poetry, and also given that I could imagine no better guide into hell. Built like a Viking warrior, with long blond hair and a face shaved by a sandstone, he was utterly threatening. They said that steroids had fried his brain, that his real name was Noah and his family wanted to reconnect with him – but there was nothing to reconnect with anymore. Looking into the middle distance, he would talk to himself of his genius and his visions, sometimes shouting about how far ahead of everyone else he was with his ideas.

Another used to play card tricks to whoever was passing, but he would always make a mistake and the card tricks never worked. I wondered whether that was part of the trick, to get the audience to sympathise and give him money anyway. Like with Mushroom Ed, as soon as he started to talk about giving him money, people made excuses to leave, which is something I also did. I never found out his name sadly; he wore a top hat and his eccentric appearance became a clue for people to recognise him and then immediately cross the street.

There was a veteran who sat every day on a bench, his face red and decaying from alcoholism and sunburn. Some days he dressed as a country gentleman, others in a frayed football shirt, but always with a can of beer in his hand. His bench was situated by a bus station and he amused himself by capturing an audience of lost tourists into inconclusive conversations. I don't think he liked me: as if he were on to what I was doing, he would grumble things that I couldn't hear but sounded unfriendly. At that bus stop, there was graffiti scrawled onto the seats: *Fuck refugees. Fuck gays. Fuck students.* I checked myself when I realised that I had automatically assumed it was the veteran who had written this message, as a seething need to communicate with everyone without being questioned afterwards. I only ever spoke to the veteran once: I was asked the time and then found myself in a meandering lecture on how methadone is no good and a menu of drugs should be available on the NHS: I agreed.

***

These searches reminded me of someone I once knew. He was one of those folks you hear glimmers of from various people you thought were unconnected, yet somehow they all triangulate on an area, thing or, in this case, a person. Hearing him through other's voices, I couldn't help but want to fill in the gaps in their knowledge of the man, to give the context it appears only I knew of. To many of them, I think he was little more than a strange man, someone amusing to tell stories of but would rather avoid in the flesh. Perhaps that is why I had been thinking of him more regularly of late – to provide some sense of reparation.

Not long ago, I was told by one of those inexplicable mutual friends that he had been found crying, wailing almost manically apparently, to the police, demanding they return the carcass of a badger he was in the process of skinning, to tan its fur and somehow use it. Someone must have been peeking from behind the fancy curtains of their safe little home and later spoke of the crazy man with the animal and a knife on their street. The police warned him that he could have been arrested for animal cruelty, though a cursory glance at the animal would have shown that a car had killed it and he did not own a car. Nobody knows what he was planning on using the dead badger fur for; nobody has heard from him since. Disappeared back into the woods from whence he came, some say. But that is not true, no. He, in fact, came from a very wealthy middle-class family, the only child of very proper parents. Hearing that, some people were surprised that he was not found swaddled in the great black forests or carried away by a river and eventually raised by wolves, or whatever ridiculous excuse for his way of living they could think of. I would visit his house occasionally when we were younger as we used to go to the same after-school clubs and became friends of a sort. Even back then, he always seemed spaced-out, though he did not smoke until much, much later – you must understand that the village he lived in was very conservative. In fact, most of the time when people spoke of him, they couldn't tell the difference between whether he was high or not; I reckon there was roughly a fifty-fifty chance either way.

I remember the one time his parents were out of the house, on holiday or something, and I came round and almost immediately he set off for the woods. He had stolen some spirits from the cupboard and put them in a small jar, and although we drank it almost immediately, it was not enough to lay us out. We built a fire – a bivouac – and spoke long into the small hours. What we spoke of, I do not remember. The next day, his parents were able to somehow decipher that he had taken some of the booze and although they said nothing in front of me, you could see the outrage in their eyes. I was never invited back again. And from then on, I only heard of him via others – that said, I did once see him on the street. He had grown a beard by then and I almost did not recognise him. He was part of a commune and looked content with life. I was told that he had taken to a passion for whittling spoons out of wood. I then remembered an earlier tale that he had attempted a brief spell as a carpenter's apprentice, but making things to order had not fitted well with him. What he did with all those spoons of varying quality, I have no idea. I suppose they must have been given away or else abandoned. Perhaps he branched out into other crafts, for it seems that the latest interest is tanning. Not himself – tanning animal hide. Then what, after that? A spider's web of festivals and squatting in various buildings, subsequent evictions, rumours of joining a circus, partaking in those New Age druidic mystical gatherings to celebrate solstices – that kind of thing. And each time, the tone of the speaker got ever more sceptical concerning his mental health. But if you ask me, I do not think there was – *is*, for he is still alive as far as I know – anything wrong with him. Even for me, it is all too easy to place him in the past tense; one hears about that way of life and assumes it can only have a certain and very limited duration. Prejudice, that's all it is.

I digress. I do not even think it can all be put down to "rebelliousness" either; he never thought in terms of antagonisms, not even with his parents, and I assume he still drops in on them from time to time. The idea that someone disapproves or thinks differently to him, I reckon he considers an accident, like a duff move in a chess game. Even now, after the badger incident, I don't think it even occurred to him that the whole enterprise would have looked off-kilter in a residential area of town, late at night and seemingly in the open on the street. No, I think I even admire him for being that particle of chaos in a world of terms and conditions, one-way streets and company investments; the world where the hour of 6am exists. Where he is now, I do not know, but I like that he is out there somewhere. The last I heard of him, he was somewhere in the far north or the western islands, though I can easily imagine him roaming south to one of the home counties and reclaiming some land for his own from a lord's grounds. He never needed to read Rousseau or Marx. Long live the nomad king, I say. Long live the badger-skinner.

***

I walked past a man having a seizure and watched in the

distance as others helped; I avoided the eye of charity collectors; I was spat on. These were just a few disparate events that suddenly occupied my life. When the man was dying, I wondered as I crossed the street how I should watch the event, whether to watch like a journalist presumably would or how one absent-mindedly watches pornography. I smiled when I saw how people would fully extend their arm to touch the dying man's shoulder while still maintaining an effective distance. Some people came, stayed for a few minutes, then, realising their dead weight, slowly walked off, trailing backwards glances to check whether the scene had changed.

When I avoided the eye of charity collectors, I raced through all the things I could say to them, such as asking them exactly *for what* they gathered alms for, and thereby intend to prolong. Help us defeat cancer – for what? Help us raise money for war-torn countries – for what? Had they not heard life is an aberration that never quite contains its immutable desire to return to inert matter? And then they would stare at me stupefied and I would walk on by, mentally counting the curses that silently flew through the charity worker's head.

And when I was spat on, I did not know that it had happened at first. I did not know the person – I had never even seen him before – and just stood there momentarily paralysed, before turning around and swearing at the person, who was, himself, swearing back at me. It was, I somehow knew, very deserved: I should be spat on. Once the impotent rage subsided, I found myself realising that I felt alive, that I had not been taken for one of the living dead; like that sensation of when I was exhibited upon, there was a similar transformation into an unsuspecting glee. I had been wrenched from myself more violently than before and the world and its objects hummed vibrantly for a day.

***

At the supermarket where I shopped, there was always someone there filming me and whoever was on the street. She was not a student with some odd film study in mind, nor did she work at the supermarket, but she was always there. The way she made eye contact was unnerving and, as the weeks went by, I could not help but notice that she singled me out for her film, continuing to stare long after I had disappeared inside. It was like I had become a suspect; she saw me as somehow being the threat, that perhaps I was an undercover policeman. This experience made the supermarket become unreal to me, a sickly lighted knot of excessive things, until I had the thought that one day supermarkets might die out and then where would the woman go? One day, she disappeared and I felt dimly sad; I wondered at an affinity towards her, wherein she, too, was a witness to the end of things.

***

Here, it is worth recalling a different dream. The effect in this dream felt somehow pre-empted, that I knew it was going to happen long, long before it ever did, and this simultaneously surprised me and did not surprise me. It went like this: I waited at a window, staring over rooftops until a tiny red light descended like a falling aeroplane.

There was an indeterminate pause and then grey, billowing shockwaves turned the blue sky black and thunderous. Strangely, I felt little despair as the explosion threw me. There was almost no violence in the force of the explosion it seemed. Alive, I found a broken mirror to pick the glass shards from my face.

An anticlimactic end, perhaps, but the dream set apocalyptic thoughts running through my mind. How many would kill themselves when they realised it was happening – *really happening*? This little society of ours cannot go on indefinitely; none ever does. It would creep over and finger each body and then they would *know*. I reasoned that nobody believed in the apocalypse, except only myself and the woman at the supermarket. If they all believed it, no one would allow for all this to exist: there would be riots on the streets, riots of fear. Their homes are stuck in the middle of the desert. They just do not believe it yet. Maybe when the public information documentaries are broadcast, they will. They provide the facts; the superhero apocalypse films provide the graphics at the centre. Then, the slow rot as the centre collapses and the refugees huddle towards the remaining greenery. Beheaded, the fingernails keep growing. I'll be dead by then.

***

There was something relentless in everything that passed my restless gaze; it itched. After seeing and recording so many bent legs and charred faces, old men clutching the sides of buildings with their wrinkled penises poking through their flies, and almost being punched in the face by an American tourist wildly gesticulating, I thought about purchasing a hunting knife. Some maniacal weapon against a maniacal world. This decision was confirmed when I witnessed a bank advertisement on a billboard: a hand, with puppet strings tied around the fingers, loomed into the face of the viewer and the text read:

WHEN AN ABUSER CONTROLS YOUR FINANCES, THEY CONTROL YOU.

The message was clear and I immediately began research on where hunting knives could be bought. I found out that I had to get another person to sign off that I was not going to use the knife for murderous or terroristic purposes. There would have to be a legitimate excuse for wanting one: I imagined saying something vague about camping and thinking it important that I learn how to look after myself in the wilderness. Of course, the knife was not meant to be used against anyone specifically; I just wanted to have one, as one would hold a secret, as a physical reminder of my complicity with the shape of the world. I would not take it outside with me; I would not threaten the police with it. It would be tucked away in a drawer in my desk – an icon, a statute. It would balance a world of two-for-one meal deals, of plastic and delirious department stores, of breakfast cereals with unaccountably happy cartoon characters on the box covers. The hunting knife would be like the forgotten manifesto in its own way, but, in the end, I never bought one.

***

I was, and perhaps still am, trying to evince the impossibility of living heretofore: the existence of a latent mania.

***

A fable: *Considering the imminent closure of their island and the annihilation of themselves as a population and a culture, the islanders held council. The debate was split: half argued that they should continue the struggle to last as long as they possibly could under the memory of the stars they thought to be eyes; the other half argued in favour of pooling all the remaining resources to hold a massive carnival for the whole island. The latter half were eventually derided and persecuted into finding themselves the condemned minority. Their heresy consisted in the notion that their celebrations of the life of their people would effectively culminate into a collective suicide as the end progressed. Clandestine celebrations were held, however, to the righteous fury of those funerals held above ground. The island decayed; people died. No more calendars were printed because they became acutely unnecessary...*

***

There is an airport not far from where I live. From my window, I can see them taking off, flying over three towers that are reminiscent of the old architectural designs for the Friedrichstrasse Skyscraper project: three claws bared against the sky, sharp, geometrical, looking as if they were carved straight out of the rock with glass fused into them. Gathering speed, the airplanes sound as if they are in pain. And if it is a day where the clouds hang low in the sky, they flicker in and out of view, and then, in that moment, they appear almost alive, until they disappear and are never seen again. There are times when I wonder what it would be like to witness an aeroplane fall from the sky. I recognise the immorality of the daydream; it does not stop me thinking it.

**

I do not speak to many people. Occasionally, I get a word in, and those that listen longest evince a sympathy of sorts. I remember someone saying with much hesitancy that what I thought I was witnessing in this unacceptable landscape bared some likeness to the sanity of a doomsday preacher. That is: mad to look at, but, given the premise, the conclusion was profoundly logical. The preacher becomes sane to the point of madness when the voluptuousness of reasoning arises from the surety of hell…

Later, long after our conversation had passed, I thought it was more like receiving signals in the dark, which I plotted on a graph just to see if a logic of its own would present itself. What she had said also made me think of paranoid detectives, not just content with the fact or event of the crime, but its idea, of turning it into the Idea, with a consciousness of its own, and I saw these lost souls going mad and savagely flicking through empty pages with the lights turned down low, looking for explanations.

We met again by accident a few weeks later and she said that she had been thinking more about what I had said, although without any pleasure, and thought that to get the point she should aim with less accuracy and learn to run the spasmodic corridors, gorge dizzily, become inhuman... but these thoughts were repugnant and made no sense and she felt the temptation into madness. I have not seen her since and I think she is avoiding my company now.

***

I had taken to wandering around in public, imagining what it would be like to have a hunting knife or some such absurd weapon in a backpack. I realised that merely standing around as others looked at timetables or judged clothing while I held a hunting knife in my bag would give myself terrific scope to witness the meaning of commitment towards everything that is given automatic reverence. Going through train stations, I heard on repeat:

If you see something that doesn't look right,
speak to a member of staff or contact transport police.

I was engulfed by the fact that they were now talking about me, yet they did not know it. Watching the trains leave and the people haggard and faceless move on and on, I wondered what would happen if people began to eye me suspiciously. 'Report! Report!' they cried, but no one knew where to look. What was suspicious? In short, everything, when you know the Weimar Republic is almost over. And then you go into the parks, and then you think you see everyone with guns and blades and malice and horror in their faces. The shops are selling – *but what are they really selling?* Told to have a critical mind at school, they'll make the kiddies suspicious of everything. Critical of what? Perhaps of the great glass towers hovering overhead like an alien colossus, here so long that we have forgotten our occupation.

I then found a perfect place to witness while with the knife: loitering around obscenely paid office buildings. The conveyer belts of offices, telephones, printers, computers, ties and the illusion of worthwhile productivity made for jaded company. Being idle while they worked so hard for something no one knew of reminded me of what St. Thomas Aquinas said about heaven: that one of the greatest pleasures the saved could savour would be to watch the torments of the damned. Perhaps they were all lizards after all; maybe the rumours are true… Perhaps they will get to Mars, but I could not quite figure out a point to that endeavour. There is nothing up there, but it will nonetheless serve as an expansion of territory. *Who owns the Moon?* I wondered and then remembered that it was possible to spend money so that someone, a friend or a loved one, can have a star drifting through the universe named after them and that becomes the official name astronomers use. How insane must the person who came up with that idea have been?

Often, I think that St. Thomas and I would have found a lot in common; perhaps I should have become a priest. It was like an atmosphere over everything; they all do it, going here, there, hustling, buying, selling, working, doing it again and again, hardly sleeping, and then they die at some point and then presumably it's all over. Clearly, they must believe in heaven or, at least, that their name will live on in the form of some star that humanity will never reach. They must believe in heaven, even those who disavow it: there would be rioting in the streets otherwise.

**

In a dream, I was watching a news presenter who was simultaneously in the flesh and on screen. She would talk, then buffer and repeat herself again and again. She then stopped and called to the producer off camera, 'They're trying to get in, they're *invading*'. I didn't know who was trying to hack into her mind, but I thought: Russians.

**

Another conversation: This is a golden age, they were saying, and there has never been a better time for humanity. In terms of comfort, never has any epoch understood it as well as ours. Granted, there are a few steps taken backwards, but, overall, we are getting less racist, less sexist and, overall, people's lives are better. That is not to say that we still have things to improve upon – I'm not arguing complacently here – but I choose my words very carefully when I say that this is the best time to be alive. What do you say? I said nothing.

**

I had more strange dreams. I watched one as if through a camera lens. A stranger had written a coded message to be delivered via telegram. A waiter at the bar oversaw them writing the message. The waiter had suspicions of the contents of the message. It was dark outside. The stranger left and they took a path through an industrial estate. The waiter decided to follow the stranger, perhaps to perform a citizen's arrest should they have felt it indictable. They got to a bridge that crossed a motorway and, on the other side, there were giant concrete monuments. The path took them through two rectangular murals, the entrance engraved with images of owls – Bosch's owls. The stranger knew that the waiter was following him; he reached the owls just as the waiter climbed the bridge and turned around to look directly at the waiter. He pointed at him.

Time had passed. The stranger's hand was cut. It was tropically raining. He ran again into the dark bar and pushed his way past a crowd of damp figures and anonymous shouts and into a bathroom. In the dream, there was one especially loud, violent-looking figure who dominated the place. His clothes were all broken somehow – not torn, ripped or ruined, but *broken* – and some of the darker patches looked like blood. Slipping into a cubicle that had become transparent, the stranger noticed that he was looking at him – the stranger was an unknown face and therefore suspicious. He washed his hands and pulled the flush to make everything sound normal. As soon as he came out, the violent-looking man was there, threatening the stranger and saying that he had broken his glass, and that he had to pay for it.

Then the scene extended and I saw in the dream

that couples began congregating, and started to touch each other, slowly turning into an orgy. One woman masturbated another through her underwear; two other women, hand-in-hand, went into the cubicle the stranger had just left. The booths filled with bodies. The stranger had to step over fucking bodies and, in doing so, accidentally knocked over and broke a glass. The violent figure screamed at the stranger and they fought, then I saw the stranger twisting this violent-looking man's head round and round as if his neck was elastic and eventually drop him to the ground.

***

Every day I went out, I saw the same helicopter flying overhead. A billionaire, a flying enthusiast, the police. Thin, stick-like, it endlessly circled as if trying to escape the sky itself. *But no, that was a mistake*, I thought. It silently wanted the ground, pawed over it, staring at the earth: its flight was a continual falling, a jump downwards. What did it *see*? It reminded me that I had noticed other things like it: I noticed black cars that would suddenly accelerate and wail and flash blue: an unmarked police car. And as soon as I had seen one, I caught sight of many more. Perhaps it was the area I happened to live in, but mine was a typically WASP neighbourhood. There are suddenly a lot of unmarked police cars – how many? With that, I realised I was witness to the city's secret police and I wondered whether this had all been so sudden. Perhaps they had always been there, only I was never looking to see them. I remembered the witnessing in front of the office buildings and wondered whether we had been observed all along; whether they knew about the plans for buying a hunting knife and conspired to make such a purchase impossible – and if they did, if they knew, what is to be done?

***

I have been masturbating every day.

***

Consider the car parks. Overlooking the tarmac and concrete, I formed my own little proof for the non-existence of God: it was all too banal for an omniscient mind to have thought of. It lacks erudite theology, nonetheless I feel that the spirit of the proof holds.

***

The remains of forest fires have become tourist attractions. A twenty-something-year-old was doing a vlog about it. On top of a sand dune with tourists milling about, they had erected a walkway made of wood with steps for easy access to take photographs of mangled trees and debris. A café served cool beverages and smiles. A tourist information board told you what you could see from the top. The car park had been expanded and they had also built a coach park for school trips and for the holidaymakers from further afield. Some took their pictures next to a thermostat, showing them withstanding the heat with smiles all round. The background: miles of charred trees until you could not see for the grey haze that became the vanishing point of the camera's vision. It is unclear whether the sense of being on holiday was at all upset by the surrounding environs in which the holiday was taking place. One cannot have faith in the youth once you have met them.

***

A cyber security company tells me: *Don't just manage identities. Secure them.* Not only am I to be managed but secured, too. Securely managed.

***

'*It has always been my dream to help people with their finances. I am hoping to open up my own accountancy practice with my* **BSc (Hons) Accounting and Financial Management**' – Jotlana, 40.

I laughed aloud when I read that on the underground. People looked at me funny.

***

I went out on the hunt for conspiracy theorists: why not? I needed entertainment and I had not found a good book to read. Many of them were over sixty and had lodged themselves into student societies or other rather innocent social groups. There, they would soon establish a reputation for denying the Holocaust or believing in some other conspiracy, and then make attempts to speak publicly at a conference. The youngest of those conspiracy theorists had been around thirty and, through a series of conclusions brought about by the persistent viewing of online videos, she had argued at length how the pyramids at Giza and the Mayan temples were conduits of alien energy. I now regretted that I had only heard of the lecture after the fact, as rumours and bad retellings.

Another one of them I thought was still around, someone who owned a junk shop that had been banned from several student societies, from both the right and left wings. I made note to try and find him. I asked around and many of those I asked raised their eyebrows uncomprehendingly for why I would try to look for such a man. When I eventually found the tiny number of students who knew who he was, they told me that he had died the winter before. He, too, had now passed over into legend. Delighted that someone had come to consult them, the students who knew him would reminisce his stories and a couple even recollected a drinking game they had developed around this person. The game was simple and personal: whenever he would mention his thesis that Marxism was a branch of fascism, or his involvement with spiritualism via hallucinogenic drugs, or the merits of homeopathy, or began his sentences once again, 'No, no, no, no, no, no, no, no, the thing is, is…', you drank. In short, it was a shame the game could no longer be played.

Another theorist was called Paul Thompson. He even went so far as to invite me around to his for dinner one evening. When I arrived at his house, my politeness caught in my throat on seeing a peroxide blonde wife, whose name I never learnt, alongside this very small and grey man set amid geometrical wallpaper, seemingly designed to produce epileptic fits. It was as if the wallpaper was compensating for an energy that should have been within his body. I secretly wished that some other people were joining us, but no one else came. That was a night to behold: everything moving too slowly to be normal, while the walls themselves came alive and sent vibrations through your feet, up through your legs until they parroted your voice. Over the months following that evening, I wondered whether Paul had suffered from some sort of schizophrenic catatonia and I am still unsure. Yet I could never bring myself to feel sorry for him – even after I heard that he and his wife (name still unknown) had separated. Or that they hadn't separated, but they lived in different parts of the house. Testimonies contradicted each other and no one seemed to want to ask Paul himself. I wished Paul would save himself by getting drunk and shouting at old ladies in bus shelters – something that would stand as an equivalent to my imaginary hunting knife.

I began to develop my own personal legend around Paul, too: that he did not breathe through his nose and mouth. I imagined him with a funnel system built into the back of his head. His grey eminence had to be supported by some machine simply because the way he sighed a greeting was not a human timbre, but the reverberations of a funnel shifting gear. And when it did shift gear, I imagined that the Funnel Man encountered his fractal selves, which greyly emanated as dim sounds around him. And on these alternative frequencies, there were strange elevations and pitches screaming through the white noise, making visitations upon other Paul Thompsons slouching on different planets. Paul Thompson had once been a university professor, but was asked to leave after some unacademic theories. Knowing this gave way to thinking abstractly about Thompson's former students and I remembered how I had hated being one myself. After all the classes and all the essays, I knew that the chances were that they would have a consultancy career and plenty of pills, and that if they had depression, then it would be rational and not necessarily clinical. There was no counselling in the face of administrations that put numbers against the quality of one's thoughts, nor for the predictability of a life that logically follows since birth. Everything gets swallowed up.

I saw this also in the geography of the city, where it appeared that hardly any of the buildings had anyone dwelling in them. A few cafés, restaurants, bars, a supermarket – all compressed against layers of offices, cubicles and computers, with white light crystallising everything into clear unbridled reality. (I have always hated the bright white light often used in offices because – even though I have never been – it reminds me of Guantánamo Bay.) Work's echo was in everything, and I shivered to think of what it must be like to wake up each morning and look across the street and see your office in a parallel building to the one you slept in – the convenience of it all was too galling. A life where one never has to leave the square mile that denominates sleep, work and consumption, like a village recreated within a city. And then, like St. Thomas, pleasure grew at not being that person. I looked out across the river and saw even mightier buildings, skyscrapers, and remembered one New Year's Eve when the towers exploded with fireworks and I had the barely supressed wish that one of them should miss their intended trajectory and career into the glass, somehow setting it alight and burning down the banker's paradise. I again had to gather my equanimity from the thought and tried to detach myself from it – it was just resentment speaking. I looked again and saw how beautiful they were. Over the shoulder of their metal corners, the sky burned blue and my gaze lingered into its infinitude. Perhaps my face even unknowingly curled into a sublime smile as if I were overwhelmingly happy at something. Regardless, I began to feel a detachment from earth for staring so long. I recalled a conversation with someone who could not look at tall buildings for too long because seeing the sky behind it made her feel vertiginous, like she was going to fall into space, and I thought that the prospect was maybe not so bad after all.

The university Thompson had worked with had seemingly already had a premonition of the way things were headed: even though student suicides had increased, I read on the news that it had stopped publishing the figures, telling the public there was no correlation between its mechanism and death. These proclamations reminded me of Virgil: I had seen Virgil stride the street bellowing that they would make the students feel like throwing themselves off cliffs: 'You're going to go home crying about shitty shithole and the mental health clinic will be overflowing thanks to shitty shithole!'. *Yes*, I thought, *one day we'll watch them all jump off. They will cure themselves of the world the past generations made by finding the cure to life, in their cubed room with the curtains drawn and the door locked. Meanwhile, for the rest of us, it is getting too expensive to live with our sunken investment society.*

***

For respite, I would take long walks along the riverbank. The river lapped close against the path at high tide and, in some areas, I could see where the river had spilt over the barriers. There is a map I once saw online of the projected cityscape in thirty years' time or so: all that stretch of land would be under water. And not just that area, but miles behind would be totally effaced and, in its wake, there would lie instead a delta. In thirty years' time or so, my flat will have a "river view", which would really be a sight of a congealed floating mass of debris and sinking buildings. In a further year or two, maybe three years, the flat would become part of the delta as well. Yet "For Sale" signs feverishly dotted that stretch of path, advertising the steel and glass properties, and I wondered whether those potential buyers had seen the projected maps. Those maps are not a common sight; perhaps money had changed hands to keep it that way.

Over the weeks, I tallied some of the items I saw washed up at low tide. They were as follows: a massive log, millions of pieces of detritus of unpacked food, cellophane, wrappers, a drawer from a metal filing cabinet, an electric bike that had been thrown overboard and was slowly being fossilised in the clay and a dead cat. I noticed that people would calmly wander along the brackish strand at low tide and on seeing the cat's corpse, they instantly recoiled back into the world estranged from their daydreams and hastily retraced their steps and pretended they never saw such a thing as death by drowning. What I saw sedimented my imagination and yet produced an ambivalent effect of a growing nonchalance in the face of all good people who smile benignly and say, 'Why should all this come to pass?'. The virtual space of the sheer weird was continually entering into me like Borges' kingdoms in the mirror slowly unbinding themselves from their image to invade the real world.

***

I began to worry that maybe these thoughts I was having about the world were the thoughts of a fascist. Indeed, this seemed confirmed when I walked past a bus station with scrolling advertisements for the bus-catchers to watch while they waited. On one of the scrolls, I paused, not sure if I had read the slogan properly. I thought I had read, "Rommel: London" with a curvaceous woman wearing red lipstick and pouting. *No, it can't be*, I thought. When it came around again, I corrected myself. It read "Rimmel", not "Rommel". Of course – why would it be otherwise? Why on earth would they name a cosmetic brand after the Nazi general? Then I imagined if a cosmetics company went fully for it, grasping the punters by naming something so outlandish it would gain publicity from the sheer controversy. Like naming it "The Fourth Reich" or something mad. This is where my brain goes in search for associations: Nazi Germany. I should be shot where I stand.

***

I wanted to save myself. I wanted to save myself and at least a few others – those who deserved to live, having done no harm to others. I imagined an island garden to place them on, not unlike Easter Island, although it looked more like those coastal landscapes I used to visit as a child. It would be a small paradise to weather the slow, habit-ridden collapse of all the lives I saw around me. A little shed, like a beach hut, built at the top of an inaccessible cliff, or a horse and cart to nomadically wander north as the southern deserts expand and entire continents become uninhabitable. Even now, I look forward to the time when there is no more oil to fuel the cars and horses reappear on the roads and bring back with them a sense of voyage – the same can be said of sailing ships. In my mind, the list of human beings I would save multiplied and divided, was subtracted to a miniscule number, only to balloon to the size of a garden city. Then I thought of the people I left outside its walls: what would it mean to save the likes of Paul Thompson, the Funnel Man? But it was no use helping it, for Thompson was definitively numbered among the fucked. Almost everyone was labelled among the fucked and more kept on being added to the list as more were born. Regardless of how monied one was, if there was some fatal monotony that stank like death around them, they were herded into the camp.

And as for myself? I had imagined myself in that shelter, a little tent against the tide, but that was because I was the witness. I was – as everyone imagines themselves in the apocalypse – among the survivors. None of it was real, I consoled myself, so if I put myself on the magical spaceship, then it hardly mattered. I knew, quite transparently, these daydreams were both hopelessly idealistic and ruthless, although I suspect they are shared with plenty of others when their mind turns to how the world is going. Either way, being a witness was enough. I would occasionally lapse into class consciousness, only to revel in the excess *schadenfreude* over the likes of Mushroom Ed later. Equally, my ability to relax and watch other people's hurried lives became easier and I laughed – not spitefully, but a kind of laugh when you see how absurd things are when they are done at double-speed or slow-motion, or seen through a glass window without any sound.

***

I took serious note of my fantasies and tried to make them more real than reality. I gained weight. Depending on who I talked to, I became militantly political, arguing for the dissolution of everything. I fantasised about being in power, being in cabinet, being prime minister, being a renegade MP who shouted and screamed. Then those daydreams would sink with all my other aspirations and I would conclude that there are no politics we could achieve, and I increasingly liked the idea of sharing a tent with Mushroom Ed. Humanity cannot be saved and does not want saving – saving to what end? The world has its own problems. In lieu of a praxis, I appealed to a simple law of thermodynamics: for every action, there is an equal and opposite reaction. On TV, I would watch the ministers produce increasingly violent sound bites and cheered with obscene glee as the increasingly stupid and intolerant politicians won seats and ruled the country. I became an arsonist of the mind.

**

It all appeared confirmed that I was not the only one when, passing by, I saw something strange in a homeowner's garden. The welcome mat at the bottom of their door faced the door and did not spread the message out towards the world for anyone coming into the house. "Welcome" was, therefore, not addressed to anyone entering the house; "Welcome" addressed those leaving the house.

Fear of the world, I thought. A mistake, an unknowingly known mistake. A message to themselves; anxious of what's out there – justified, no doubt – they've sent themselves the comforting message of welcoming: "Welcome to the world. You belong here." Yes, they, too, thought a little bit like me.

**

To my surprise, I found that I would unknowingly take up strange seating positions. Resting my arm over my head with my hand dangling by my ear – like a forgotten pose that ancient painters utilised, but without the grapes dangling to the lips of naked Roman women – I would feel myself slowly slouch further into the chair, my clothes riding up on me as if they were automatically undressing. I would fiddle with things around me. Once, I realised how odd I must look when I broke pieces off a chair in a café by playing with it.

***

I haunted the city and never once was I recognised. Up
and down, at all hours, any street, any hour. If someone
happened to walk near me, I always looked at their face
and lived in the fraction of instants when our eyes met
– then, gone. On too many occasions I looked up and
automatically had to do a double take because I thought
it was someone I recognised. Then I would relax, wander
and pass by strangers, unnoticed and not seeing anything,
and then someone I knew really would appear, this
time in reality, as if I had been caught out, and I tried
to pretend that I had not seen them. The beauty of this
long, unmapped life had been that I was seldom taken
by surprise by people I knew. The city was large, after all,
and I walked at times when a different crowd came out.
Similar looks, certainly, but no one identical. I could move
through endless days and nobody would talk. When the
fancy took me, I stopped for a while among the crowd,
leaned against a wall and watched, or else found a bench.
My mind would remember everything I saw without my
knowing it, from the gait of their walk and the nest of
wrinkles around their eyes, to the face they pulled as the
bus drove past them.

Sometimes I would get a jump and think that I had
recognised someone from long ago, and all my calm
people-watching would fail at once. The faces of those
I once knew again appeared and would deaden all my
senses immediately, until their faces would disappear
behind others, then magically reappear, and I realised as
they came closer that they might have more make-up on

than they characteristically wore for example, and then they were ten feet away and shorter than they were, and my heartbeat slowed when I realised that it actually was not them at all, but an incredible lookalike. With all its variations, this repeated itself, although this was not entirely distressful.

***

Passing through on the underground, I soon became bored staring at the advertisements not made for anyone like me in mind. My eyes passed again over the stops gone by and those yet to come, even though by now I have the subterranean map memorised.

Next to me, a woman was reading the free newspaper – the same newspaper that lines the streets and corridors at the end of every day, matted with damp and residue, and is generally treated with contempt – and I started reading over her shoulder. Politics: something about conflicts of interest with ministers representing corporations in government. Sport. Gossip. Crossword. Something else about a beach read and how a contract had been signed to turn the novel into a TV series.

Soon, she realised what I was doing and kindly moved the paper so that I could read better. Then, she started talking to me. She said what she thought about what we were reading; I agreed with what she said and tried to make some insightful comment of my own, but the noise of the tube scraping through its hole swallowed it up. She told me that she was a comedian on her way to a gig. I asked her what her shows were like and she said that a lot of it was improvised. A few anecdotes tried and tested, but aside from that it was up to the crowd to keep the energy going. And what do I do? I dodged the question. She then unscrewed her flask and said that it wasn't water in there if I wanted to partake. Why not? The unknown spirit warmed me through and suddenly I became chattier. I think we surprised ourselves, talking to strangers in public, although maybe it was the booze that helped. Then it was her stop and we smiled to each other as she got up to leave. The doors took their time to open and, for a few seconds, we just waited awkwardly. The doors opened and someone else sat down beside me. Then, the solitude reasserted itself. It had been nice.

***

I decided to head towards the coast on a weekend, spent an hour with my toes in the sea and breathing the ocean breeze. The slowness of everything greatly appealed to me and I realised this was the first time I had felt truly calm in months. I stared lazily into the horizon. I wondered whether it was possible to buy a beach hut here. Then I would retire and live in the shack, even in winter. I would have meagre possessions. A few books, a camping stove, a mattress or sleeping bag. I would grow a beard and, still, no one would recognise me. I even considered how difficult it would be to start a small paddle and boat business, something for the summer to provide some income to occasionally go to a café or buy chips. In the winter months, I'd find some manual job, like working on the roads or on a construction site. I sat content with my hands buried deep in the sand; when I got up, I bought an ice cream for myself, deliberately choosing the one with the most colours, while thinking that selling ice creams could also be another career possibility. While eating, I almost wished for a bucket and spade. Or a line to go crab fishing like when I was a kid. Hunt crabs and sell them to the local restaurants – that was another idea I entertained about this possible life. Weimar could fall, but the beaches would stay the same. Then, as if on cue, an empty plastic water bottle floated towards me and blotted everything that I could see. My vision became that plastic bottle. The news came back to me: the water companies had dumped raw sewage into the seas and the entire coastline was contaminated. Not only had I been wading through human shit, but also the traces of antidepressants and anti-anxiety pills that had been proscribed en masse in what I saw as an apparent attempt to drug everyone into a false sense of functionality. I looked at my still wet feet and legs to disgustedly check whether they had telling tidemarks. They didn't, but I felt gross all the same. Pouring sand over my legs and then rubbing them, I hoped to get some of it off me. My equanimity had evaporated into imagining violent things done to the company executives, those who clearly must have no soul, it seems – who have no aesthetic sense whatsoever; who accrue money and do nothing with it other than buy cars, plastic and property. Bastards. Bastards! No, there was nowhere that would allow me to remain unmolested. I quickly pulled on my socks over my sandy, clinging feet, hastily tied the laces and fled back to the city. (Much later, I also learned that beach huts are far more expensive than I ever realised: some of them went for over £50,00, which may as well have been in the millions as far as I was concerned).

***

I was driving far beyond the speed limit and the motorway spat a fly onto the windshield. I mechanically wiped it away, but the fly's body smeared and stained along the screen. I thought it was strange that there was only one; there used to be thousands that would machine-gun the car when I was younger. Now, there was only one. A vertigo exposed itself and, for an instant, the gulf of everyone's death broke across my mind and anxiously terrified me. No one could hide from it; it would capture all souls – even the billionaires, who would take off quickly enough, but would eventually crash back down to earth as their technology failed them. *My God*, I thought, *we haven't long left.*

I took my mind to the greenery pushed aside by the concrete and thought about how many people on how many roads look on from the pavements, watching the cars go by. And if they were watching, were they eyeing the drivers with hatred for having to breathe in the fumes? Everyone has looks of hate, spoiling for a fight – even reasonably violent people, unaware of their violent work; the justifiers, the legislators – from the sides of the road, from any window overlooking the streets below or from the vehicles themselves. I watched the cars at rush hour – many of the drivers were on their phones and would be startled into driving again by the impatient horns behind them. Some would try to overtake and then get caught as an accelerating car opposite them stalled at an awkward angle. It was a good place to watch human psychology in action: scratching each other's eyes out to save twenty minutes getting to the motorways like rats in a barrel – all for racing to the next red light – and those whose parents lived with songs of love in the car now listened to songs of hate:

I'm doing great without you, I just wanted to say that I hate you.

Who listens to songs with lyrics like these? This sudden *volte-face* in things, the turning towards aggression, resentment, spite. It was like there had been an unacknowledged morbid birth of justified silent wrath, breeding generations of anthropophage hereafter; deranged humans unable to comprehend anything of paths laid down before them, who died raging like cattle in an abattoir from drinking the seas that we, ourselves, poisoned. I slowed down. When I arrived home, I stayed in the car for some time, surveying the road in case I had been followed.

***

I dreamt that the sky was yellow, dotted white with stars, and the sea was black. A city was to be crushed under a black tidal wave. For some reason, I was obsessing over the second-to-last prophet's name. The ancient name of the prophet I already knew (awake, I looked it up and found out that in Islam, the second-to-last prophet was Īsā – Jesus – though I have no idea where this theological knowledge came from). I had somehow translated it into its modern equivalent; it turned out to be a name I recognised, but I cannot remember what that name was. Regardless, it was too late – the tidal wave came and I only escaped by hitching a ride in a blue car with a man and his son, both of whom were utterly unknown to me. Then, we were in green hills, recovering. Floods came. Me and a group of strangers were climbing up a valley slope to escape the floods. The foliage was dense and high; spilling rivers made some of the group turn back on seeing others be swept away. Others turned back from the altitude, looking incredibly pale. Reaching the top, it suddenly descended into a cliff that met the ocean. Tidal waves smashed below. There were other people at the top of the cliff, staring blankly into the waves. I could see figures in the waves. People were swimming, although sometimes they looked motionless, and then they disappeared as the waves broke and smashed into the rock. And then I dreamt that I was far out to sea and everything was lit only by moonlight. The sky and the sea blended into one abyss, the stars shining below me just as they were above. The tranquility did not last: waves distorted the moon's perfect reflection and soon the sea foamed over the small boat and waves towered over me. Yet I was laughing, thrilled by the black waves – ecstatic almost. One wave, higher and more threatening than the rest, loomed over me in my small craft and I directed the boat right into it, to dive through the wave before being smashed by it. Under the wave I went, laughing.

***

Once, I was almost run over by a bus. Normally I manage to pass through streets seamlessly, as one does after living in a city for a long time. I only felt the fear after the event; my mind stalled as I read what had almost killed me: *Goebbels' Tours*. The scream of the horn had blown apart my awareness and, in that instant of reading, I accepted everything. A tour bus, with horrified faces looking down at me, shouting insults at me for ruining their views of the city. I eventually had to do a double take on the name of the bus: they surely had not named their business after the minister for propaganda. It was not "Goebbels", but "Cobbles" that had been emblazoned, with a cartoon dog as their mascot. It was another new tour company amid the thousands of others, with a fleet of buses and leaflets and people standing around handing them out to those who ignored them. The bus drove away and I watched it disappear with that cartoon dog still staring at me. I wondered whether the bus had had any intention to stop in the first place or whether it would have just left my dislocated and bloody body in the road. I really do think like a fascist. But this was also another tell-tale sign; if I had seen the name "Goebbels", then I could not have been alone. Some sort of subliminal messaging was being evoked by this company; they, too, had the same premonitions, though it had not fully realised it just yet. The fascist psychology is alive and well. Meandering around the city in endless circles, listing off the features of the building and landscape, all the while presenting to the citizenry, Goebbels, Goebbels, Goebbels. I was reminded of that similar occasion not too long ago when I had mistaken the cosmetics brand "Rimmel" for "Rommel" and felt confused as to their naming choice and at why my mind had immediately leapt to the Nazi general. Clearly, they had been ahead of me at the time and had fully endorsed that subtle nod to the fascist in all of us… these were undeniable clues: they were symptoms to a destructive way of thinking that had infested everyone. It took on surfaces and screens to blot out its reality, but screeched through in moments like this – a group hysteria on a level that extended over mere borders. I refrained, however, from mentioning these thoughts to anyone; I knew people well enough to know that they would simply baulk at my pronouncements and compare me to one of those doomsday preachers yelling at a crowd to repent. They would find a doctor to shove a box of pills down my throat and call it an ethical decision. I imagined myself atop a box in a park or standing on a bench with badly painted placards, awkwardly losing momentum halfway through my sentences, then lashing to the finish with more aggravated energy than predicted and falling weirdly silent again. Sometimes I think, however, that I could be one of the articulate ones: there have been many times in my head when I have been able to compose some of the most voracious speeches and effectively nod to the Book of Revelations without using any of the truly evocative words and beasts. But I still had no desire to speak to anyone about it. I was content to remain watching without trying to spread the word to make people realise what was around them. I felt that I had no right to intervene – after all, was not my voyeuristic witnessing an intervention in itself? Or if not an intervention, then at least an acknowledgement – and that if people really wanted change, they would fight for it with or without my aid. People do not know what they want, and even if I knew myself how to guide them, I had no authority to convince them. Or maybe they do know what they want – they want the world just as it is, the best of all possible worlds – and it just so happens to be the opposite of what I happen to want. In which case, let them carry on their party. It is the will of the people. And then, after these kinds of dismissive, almost blasé thoughts, a momentary sadness would creep over me as I realised my superfluousness, as the one on the outside of the town borders, that I was the crazy person who had these thoughts, that this was the person I had become: the one who saw Nazis on buses. Alongside all this, I remembered all the other encounters I had with people that should have taken my life in an opposite direction, away from the exhausting visions that populated my imagination. The men and woman I had wanted to follow were numerous; a backlog of erotic labyrinths that opened onto plateaus of simplicity. Day would break and it would no longer matter what I had ever said. The birds would sing their chorus and it would not matter that I had seen something buried about these times as if the mass upheavals were imminent. Outside, the morning staining the sky, and I would find myself still aimlessly wandering the streets.

***

What else is there in the yawning playground of my imagination?

***

Oh yes, I took to engaging police officers with sarcasm and, as I felt one day, with provocation. Maybe tomorrow or in a decade's time, the legislation will be passed that will allow them to punch me in the face or break my body and throw it in the river.

***

I intend to exhibit myself for what I am: a footnote of mental debris.

***

I soon realised that my memory was fast becoming a wraith, spliced with the images, memories and inclinations of a thousand others I had met in my lifetime. I saw their faces, the small details, like the curve of a shoulder, and felt in my mind the fabric that carved the outline over my old girlfriend's waist, but in those memories she never spoke. They were soundless tableaus; silent films comprised of held poses – that was all. I saw in myself a potential to love again, to care, to dwell in the world without misgivings, totally innocently, to bask in the gapless panorama of a million instants. It was possible for me to hold communion with the world and the people, and I did not truly want to pass by unnoticed, but the distance never closed and nothing ever happened.

***

At night, dressed in black leather, I would graffiti walls. I would let down car tyres, overturn bins, talk to cats. On the walls, I wrote strange slogans and poetry, all exclaiming obituaries that loosely referenced the fall of the Weimar Republic in the vein of the blind sayings of Virgil. I described krakens made of people taking bank notes to the bakers in the throes of a capsizing global economy. I stayed out almost entire nights. When I eventually came back, I would sleep fitfully for only a few hours at a time. I would dream that strange things were buzzing in the sky. They were alive and moved mechanically. Awake, I thought they bore a likeness to the figures in Magritte's painting *Le Drapeau Noir*.

This set off another dream, set at night, with a full moon and strong winds, which in turn reminded me of Paul Delvaux's *Dawn over the City*. Things were being ripped up into the air and rotting at incredible speed. Human beings aged at an alarming rate and withered while still alive. I was with my family, who all looked as if they were ten years younger than they were, and I had noticed my mother's arms had withered and twisted into stumps, like old branches of a dead tree. I started crying in the dream. As the wind blew and people were caught up in it, they became hollow and slowly became invisible, and were then wholly erased – blown away. The trees began to luminously grow a harsher shade of green, almost shining. Things levitated. I wondered whether there was anyone who could withstand the erasing powers of the wind. The cities were empty and humanity's landmarks had already been disbursed. Many people I did not recognise fled into bunkers and never came out. They sat preparing for a long wait, even though they knew that the rafters would not hold indefinitely. Some went into the wind or the forests, preferring not to die in darkness.

***

Idly at first, without any clear notion of what it was I intended to see, I would clandestinely take pictures of things as if I were stealing them. At first, it was the birds at the dawn chorus or the clamour of seagulls overhead. I did not fully know what these images signified; what was coded within them that was to unveil itself eventually when tuned in to the words I had written. Yet I took pleasure in how they somehow resonated and, for the most part, this period of my life was pleasant. There were parks; there were birds. In the park and seeing the birds, I would think of the lilies and then remember Weimar and smile as one does when one has no responsibility over matters. I remembered when, as a child, I had collections of encyclopaedias on all the animal kingdoms and would spend hours in front of a television screen watching wildlife documentaries. (One assumes now that the new documentaries are designed to induce guilt, which never quite follows through.) When I saw woodpeckers in the trees or cormorants in the river, I would think back to that time and begin to regret that I never pursued the ambition of being a wildlife photographer. That would have been a nice life. But then I would leave, and I did not know how the photographs of flashing sirens or a bus full of miserable people pulling into a station complemented the notion of the end of the Weimar Republic, or when that, itself, blurred into the memory of the moans of the girl next door with her legs wrapped around another man. I would edit the photographs to bring out their most violent colours and turn them into molten landscapes, which, to me, bled out the unacknowledged madness of everything ending.

***

Sometimes I listened into the private conversations of those walking by or in a café and I would follow a few paces behind, trying to record what they were saying using the mic on my phone to replay later that night. I would find myself laughing when I would splice a million voices on the TV by rapidly flicking through the channels, merging a politician's sound bites I had caught from the news with advertisements or soap operas. This would create bizarre scripts that went nowhere, but somehow in their forced association it all would link jarringly to create tenuous meanings like the babble of the television's unconscious. The need to record everything almost became compulsive. I wanted to record films and all the television programmes, so that it could be captured and saved – all there to be brought back to life when it was dead and Weimar over. I deliberately wanted my photographs to capture the soul of things so it might be brought back from disappearing altogether. Soon, I had rapidly built a vast library of details. However, I had not collected omnivorously, and those I kept held a special perspective that produced the effect I wanted – everything else I rejected outright. One particular detail struck me as having an especially lucid vantage point that informed everything else. It was a news story and the headline went:

**BOMB SQUAD ARE CALLED TO A&E WHERE
PATIENT TURNED UP WITH TWO-INCH-WIDE
WWII SHELL LODGED IN HIS RECTUM WHEN
HE 'SLIPPED AND FELL'.**

There was something perversely glorious to this story, as if it encapsulated the zeitgeist that I happened to be living through – this intensely masturbatory epoch. I wished I could have been at the front desk when the man came in, crouching in pain, and seen the doctor's face as they rummaged, with the bomb squad looking over their shoulder. I wished I could have seen the man's fantasies as he pushed the shell inside of him, whether there were images of Churchill or the glorious dead, who sacrificed their lives so that the population would be free to anally please themselves. The story must be one of the greatest love songs in the anthology of torpedoed minds.

***

Eventually, the meaning to all this will filter through to me – whisper like the voice of a god through the snow – and one day I will smile and realise.

***

I enjoyed hearing the solitary hum of an engine that incongruously stood out against the silence, begging the question of where it thought it was going and why at this time of night. *A policeman's question*, I thought, *and one that is truly apt to this kind of rigorous witnessing.* The engine, of course, spoke no words, nor did the spray cans and luminous designs of graffiti artists and vandals – which was what I felt I could always tell – but they spoke nonetheless, even if it was only ephemeral.

***

In the parks, I saw that crows and seagulls would eat the bin liners when they couldn't find anything inside to scavenge.

***

As I walked by, someone was muttering to themselves, 'Sick, sick… people are sick today!' I turned a street corner. 'C'mon then!' another man shouted to someone else from a bar. Everything is festive.

***

I would ride trains and buses and see everything in a lengthy panorama. Sometimes, in the underground, the carriage would squeal against the steel unto a piercing shriek and I would begin to grow afraid because it was a scream I imagined that demonic manifestations must sound like. Careering at breakneck speed, getting exponentially louder to fill all white noise of the world with its terror, to become the background of everything, the fundamental premise of the world, based on evil, and suddenly being forcefully made aware of that fact. Then, I would get off at a random station and find my way back again.

***

On one journey, I did not notice him until the journey was well underway and we were all too boxed-in to subtly change carriages at the next stop. At first, all I noticed was that he was holding onto the handrail excessively tightly. The veins all down his arm streaked blue and his hand looked welded onto the iron bar above his head. This would have been fine if that was all he was doing. However, his eyes were shut tight and as the carriage screamed through the underground, he smiled as if in a dream (I am glad those eyes stayed shut while in transit, because I do not know what I would have seen had he opened them). As the screeching got louder, however, the smile spread and mixed savagely with the contortion of the rest of his face and the increasing tension in his entire body. I had no idea what he was doing, but I soon realised that this man was having an orgasm of sorts. At that moment, I did not like the idea that we were underground together. Then at the next stop everything instantaneously reverted. He dropped his arm, stopped smiling and opened his eyes – a shocking pale blue, his eyes seemed to see beyond the walls of the station. He even moved out of the way to allow other passengers to board. He looked normal – to the point that I wondered whether I should be almost offended given what I had seen him do, because it made everything look like an unsolicited performance. Then again, he had done precisely nothing; there were so many freaks and weirdos out there, but even so…

The carriage doors closed and we were off again. This time, a man was stood opposite the Smiler – a young professional with a neatly trimmed beard and an expensive-looking jacket. Clearly, he was one of the winners in the spreading tide of gentrification. He had a nice face and I could imagine that throughout this young professional's life, people had always been saying that he's "a nice young man". A nice man, *ad nauseum*. Well, on that commute, the nice man did not have a nice time. No sooner had we pulled away than that arm instantly welded itself again to the handrail, the eyes closed and the head was raised ever so slightly, as if looking at something – like the way you see people basking in the sun. The young professional, of course, saw this transformation and looked anxiously about to see if other people had noticed. I managed to avoid his gaze by predicting he would look around in search of an unwilling ally. Finding nobody to share in what he was seeing manifest in this person next to him, he silently stared into the Smiler's face with evident perverse curiosity. That curiosity, however, recoiled back into anxiety as the Smiler began to grin widely, the lips drawing back over the gums like how a snake smiles, as if his entire jaw was dislocating out of his mouth as a separate entity. I saw the young professional attempt to take an involuntary step back, but was sharply barricaded against the closed doors of the tube and the unmoving bodies of other passengers. I didn't see his face as he hastily left the carriage at the next stop – but I wonder what he saw, that close, looking right down into the Smiler's gullet. I was not as close as he was to that ravaged grin and I wanted to get off, too, and as soon as I heard my station announced, I left without turning back.

Although I don't want to admit it, part of me was afraid that had I turned around, he would be there looking at me, watching me leave, like a mutation of the Eurydice tale, where this time Eurydice wants to leave the underworld and *will* follow you to the surface, somehow changed in the darkness and no longer what she was. Who knows where the Smiler was going or even what he was experiencing at the time. Leaving the station, I reasoned to myself that he was probably just off his face on something – people get used to this kind of thing eventually in large cities. But even so, when I remember that ride – a ride that, unlike all the others, I have not forgotten – I cannot tell whether my memory has embellished itself, but I recall the gums becoming redder as the lips withdrew to reveal finely sharpened teeth.

***

The drilling of roadworks marching into a coffee shop conversation; screeching seagulls drowning out human voices; certain phrases said in a certain way, leaden with a violence behind them; the assurances of advertisements; the things the men in ties said, when meshed with the sounds of the motorway or the jingle of the opening credits to the dead-channel programmes; or even sometimes blown together in a cacophony – all resembled the things I saw.

***

Entire conversations I had overheard would reimagine themselves in my mind as if they were being interviewed, with me asking questions that were almost answered by the original conversation. I would invent entire semi-disjointed conversations with strangers; here, the witnessing was taking place through a lens of my own making, with it nonetheless turning out no less true than before. I found it amusing. Then I developed a taste for interviews, be they fictional or real. Old folks cornered on park benches made for especially good material. They said almost anything. Tramps were good, too, and I wished I had the courage to speak to Virgil, but whenever he approached, I knew there was fire in the man's eyes and I felt he was apt to cut my head off in a single gesture, then immediately forget that I ever existed.

***

I went on a massive bender. Feeling the next day like a pig had shat in my head, I was unsure of what I had said when I was drunk. I had laughed and tried to get the others to laugh. Failing that, I remember fumbling my way to the urinals. There, it was suddenly quiet and there were human beings there, accursedly standing as if this – or what was out there, or the metaphysical situation – were normal. Had they all cracked or something? I faintly heard something from a voice I could not locate about the orgy scene in this city and how they often started in the toilets, then spread outwards onto various venues, and then it went something like: 'I'm going to an orgy on the weekend.' 'Oh, that's nice – have fun, stay safe.' I fumbled to record it and asked incoherent questions to nobody. My nausea was rising in increasing waves and at the peak trough, I felt everything going black.

When my consciousness resuscitated, I was on the floor with piss on my face. I was told that I had fainted and hit my head loudly on impact. There were lots of people milling around me who I did not recognise, glancing nervously at me, clearly unwilling to make eye contact. I felt myself being dragged down the stairs by these individuals and was relieved to feel the cool night air caress my face. People were asking me questions and I tried to quiet them with protestations that I was fine. They said that I should go to the hospital. I was told that I might be concussed. *Good*, I thought, *I'll be able to write wonderful surrealist poetry then*. So, I refused and eventually I was left alone, garbling and muttering into my shoes as I threw up.

Then, I was on a park bench, with no idea how I had got there. Paralytic, I could not move. I could barely lift my head. I knew it wouldn't be long before the dawn broke. I was glad of my isolation. Everyone had disappeared. I was glad nobody was about; I was glad nobody was witnessing me like I was. Eventually, I tried walking, but couldn't do it straight, and nor could I look to see where I was going because the brightness of the city lights burned my eyes. I tried to orientate myself. All that I could recognise around me was the entrance to a building that held a creeping financial leviathan. In my pocket, I found a lighter and, giggling, I tried to set fire to the stonemasonry. A nightguard came out, looked at me questioningly and gave me a cigarette. Smiling and smoking, I leaned back against the building I had sought to set on fire. Then, I slumped and collapsed. Nobody seemed to have noticed what became of me that night. (I still don't know how I made it home; for some reason, I woke up in the right place with no recollection of making the journey – clearly the autopilot is ingenious.)

Over the proceeding days, as I walked through the streets, I would smile in probably quite a strange way – as if I had amnesia – and glance sideways at those around me and think: *Why aren't they arresting me?* I at first avoided the financial building I had attempted to set alight, but that withdrawal soon gave way. Going up to it, I half-expected there to be more security surrounding the building, checking ID cards five paces before the stone wall. Yet when I passed it, I was almost disappointed that I had not even made scorch marks against the stone. There was no one outside; there was nothing to register that I was once a presence. Peering inside, I saw the security guard paying me no attention. I then incorporated it into my endless walks around the city, each time watching the security guard, as if trying to goad him, the building, everyone, into recognising me. Only once did the security guard look up; he clearly did not remember me.

***

With the nausea of that night, so came and went my fixation for recording details. It became sickly, all too much, disastrously excessive. It was an infinite practice: I would never become proficient in the witnessing of the death rattles of the Weimar Republic. The epic panorama of images and small recorded voices I had built sounded good against my internal monologue, because it vaguely reminded me of panoramic films, but the idea of going further filled me with inertia because films like *Man with a Movie Camera* or *Triumph of the Will* have already been made.

Then I remembered the girl outside the supermarket, recording everyone who came and left. What was she doing? Where was she now? I wished I could see what it was she had captured. I wished I could have five minutes of her time to ask her why she did what she did. Was it indiscriminate recording or were there moments that called forth for them to be recorded? She could have been looking for those persons she considered to be the guilty party – the instigators of it all. I imagined myself by the entrance, taking over her position now that she was not there, and that perhaps one of us had to be there, to be in the space, for it to make sense. I imagined the opening scenes to the film we could have made; in my area of the city alone, there were seven supermarkets to wander around as if the camera were in a hypnotic crypt, as well as the car parks that filled those supermarkets. Then, over a speaker, came the message I have heard so many times: '*Begging and soliciting are illegal. Customers are requested not to encourage this behaviour.*'

In between the supermarkets are the streets lined with charity shops and the odd coffee shop. People travel on motorised chairs with crutches strapped to the back.

***

Mine was only a small corner to view the scene, and entire universes span between horizons. So many ships passing in the night on over-expanding magnitude. Even now, objects seemed to be breaking away from my reach again, such that it felt like I was experiencing the world as if through the wrong end of a telescope. I, as Witness, seemed to have entered a tacit contract with the city that I should not be molested on any account during the Witnessing; no one must break character, nor reintroduce that reality of recognition that we are all, in some form or another, used to.

***

I began to picture in my mind the scenes that I would like to film but never would. Let others make the films; I'll stand at my witnessing post. Many of those films I imagined as being far away; conversations seen from afar that could not be audibly captured. A long-mimed soliloquy of an old man walking to the shops. Staccato of people in suits doing something incomprehensible to anyone without a tie. Perhaps at some point, the Antichrist might burst onto the scene and at least be able to explain a thing or two about where it is all headed as the hordes of Beelzebub tear away the sky. The silent chaos was becoming all too much for me. In between these imagined scenes, there would be respite at the prospect of maybe getting away, going to the sea again perhaps – the ultimate place of escape – and zoning out into the horizon like a TV. I hoped that one day there would be small underground screenings of those as-yet unmade films for the like-minded; there would, at last, be some form of community. Convert the living room into a home cinema. It was popular these days instead of going out – why not modernise? Keep in step; forwards march to victory.

***

For my own amusement, or perhaps to create some sort of blueprint, I bought a sketch pad and began to draw scenes. Yet they never resembled anything that could remotely be reproduced in film. Simple street scenes descended violently into carnivals and still lives took on a demonic edge that was not there when I gazed upon them. I laughed at them when they became accidentally comic. Objects morphed so quickly, blending into something altogether different that I sometimes had difficulty in catching up to identify what my own hand had created.

Rifling through pieces of waste paper I found, I would cut out the advertisements and stick them together. And soon, a desiccated cartoon of Humpty Dumpty became the face of breakfast cereals; a naked portrait of Samuel Beckett sat among an article reporting on genocide. I realised what I was doing was like the mad interchange of advertisements before the film at a cinema: violently loud images of white and comfortably middle-class families smiling past each other at a circus to shift into shot-at child refugees with flies in their eyes. After all, I could not describe them as storyboards, more a release of psychic nervousness. A drawing of Funnel Man anally penetrating a pig surrounded by saluting Nazis turned into a mass machine quoting unheard-of miasmas that

I had heard randomly outside. Particularly proud of that one, I stuck it on the wall. Next came James Joyce decorated in a loin cloth, which made him resemble Gandhi. Jean Baudrillard suddenly appeared with a strained neck and seemed to be communicating with strange lizard beasts that merged the anatomy of rabbits and maggots. No, none of this could be filmed – though I figured it all lay just behind what I saw around me. People's words gestured at it unknowingly.

***

I had another strange dream at around this time. I don't know why I think about it now. It was set many centuries ahead, where all humanity resided on a life-support machine the size of a hospital. They survived by cooperative rituals of cleaning, easing and moving each other. A declaration of love was to clean another body. I then saw a yellowish, clammy thing manoeuvring a transparent membrane, which had been wrapped around a tube to give it structure. The only detail that gave a tell of its humanity was its face. It was the face of a fifty-odd-year-old man, which was opposite another tube with another face – a female patient-citizen with a look of only a slight difference to tell them apart. The yellow creature started cleaning the membrane with an ice scraper. The membrane's blood vessels, which criss-crossed like a river network over the membrane, glowed red and green as if inflamed. As the ice scraper clawed along the body, the vessels burst and blood with the consistency of water smeared across the membrane, yet the inflammation receded and died down to a rusty stain. This was lovemaking in the hospital society.

***

I watched a lot of films. I omnivorously consumed everything, from the films at Cannes to whatever was on the TV in the dead hours of the afternoon. It was partly fuelled by a longing to see the world without me being there; the same could be said for books. I also watched pornography. The vast library of pornography online impressed me for its sheer volume and by being simultaneously formulaic and imaginative. Buried under there, I found a bizarrely intellectual streak in some pornographer's films: references to Picasso and Stockholm syndrome peppered the opening credits. There was clearly a difference between professional and amateur pornography, with scenes and poses designed to extract – if not eroticism – sexual magnitude, and I could not denounce it definitively as not being art. And what was it that I was doing, all this witnessing and recording – art or pornography? I thought that this will all one day pass and these thoughts will leave me cold. I will climb down from this high and see it all backwards. It will all be unfamiliar then – how to maintain an extremity of living without burning out? At last, the precariousness of being who I was right now fell through my brain, thinking about a time when I will arrest myself and walk away an old man with memories I can barely comprehend.

***

The girl at the supermarket. I wanted so desperately to find her and ask her. I needed to know whether her brain was simply fried or if she believed it had all got to end at some point. Our time, this time, the era of supermarkets. To watch the last years of people milling around the corridors with an orgy of food around them, picking and choosing, funnelled along, on and on. How fantastic! Gorge on! What a stellar enterprise! She was right to film them there, at the watering hole. Scenes of terror and stabbings were of little interest – already those thoughts were boring me. It is the jangle of trolleys, the rustle of moving products that fascinated me. It was a sick joy; one probably only explainable long after the fact, when we gaze and wonder that it ever existed at all. The staff uniforms – a crest like a banner from feudal lords, an army. And in the meantime, we are faced with unanswerable questions: what if Heinz's Real Mayonnaise was not real? What if I could not save on those massive deals? What if I could not eat well for less? What if those plums were not organic? What if every little did not help? What if people assigned their personality compatibility by which supermarket they shopped at? I'm X – then I can't be with someone from Y. New dating apps, new fetishes and infinite menagerie until it all vaporises among us, and we are left stupid and blind amid things that are losing their sense, ejected, naked and terrified.

I returned to the supermarkets, exploring them more than I ever used to. Every day, it seemed that the staff members changed, or maybe I never went to the same place twice; they changed everything, the shelves were different, the brands and colours were different, yet all based off the same fundamental premises of reassurances and faith and bargains – a kaleidoscopic illusion that nobody fails to endorse. I fondled many things, engrossed in the packaging, all the bits of plastic that were secretly destined to choke every single animal on earth. I picked up a cereal box at random. It had a massive arrow pointing towards the calorie content of the box in percentages. There were four boxes overall. Two had green; the other two were orange. The arrow had text within it, which said:

NO REDS HERE.

The cereal box's font was, however, predominantly written in red. *Ma Gawd!* My mind instantly turned. *I'm jus' lookin' at this here cereal box here an' uh can see they're lyin' to us man, they're fuckin' lyin' to us; thet 're sayin' there ain't no reds here, but uh can see 'um, and I dint know our country was so infested, so insidiously infested; it makes me want to shoot and scream and burn the Reichstag again; oh ma Gawd, I dint know that the reds were invading our supermarkets; that's a holy site of Gawd, our Gawd, and I woun't want these lil' here cereal bits gettin' in ta ma body, turnin' me red from the inside; they're tryin' to get inside me; I wou'na want be penetrated by that dirty communism; I want ma body free, patriotically free, of these invasuns, and they're on our cereal boxes, and I can see it; I've gat ev'dence raght here; I can see with ma own two eyes, ma Gawd-given eyes, on the cereal box that there are reds on ma cereal box!*

'Can I help you, sir?' How long had I been staring at this box? What must they think? Is the security near? Will I be hospitalised? 'No, thank you.' I turned and smiled.

'I'm fine.' I walked on through the maze. It is mad, all of it was completely mad for existing just like that. It was a carnival that apparently only I could see. Even then, sometimes I walked through it all automatically – go through a day having seen nothing and then realise that my vision was failing me, and one day I would see nothing, waking up blind. Perhaps then I would have an amputated happiness.

***

Walking down a street, I found a hatter. How utterly incongruous it looked, as if it had forgotten the century it inhabited. I was surprised that it still found itself a business; nobody wears hats these days. I went in, finding myself in a strange position, not knowing which way to turn and not knowing how to analyse the situation given I, too, like the rest of them, never wore a hat. Suddenly, I was immersed in all these hats in the bright shop lighting and, as I looked at them, I realised they were all facing in the same direction. Apart from the hats in the window, all the hats in the shop faced the centre of the room. I unconsciously moved into the centre and the hats became a crowd, a party, and I found myself at the centre of attention. For what purpose did the mysterious shopkeeper arrange all those hats? Each one was staring, waiting, as if expecting me to finish the toast that I had been giving for years and years. I began to have strange thoughts that if I put on one of those hats, I would finally see the faces who belonged to them. Who are these people looking at me, blurred through time, of all heights and styles of dress, of all classes, races, nationalities? It is like they had been called to meet me here in this silent shop, a clandestine space, ready as if they were prepared for a strange and unknowable exile.

***

I urge myself not to worry sometimes. And occasionally that works, but then it all comes back...

***

To pass the time, I tried to find other outlets, but reading, patrolling the streets or even listening to music had become horrible to me, and each time I tried something new, it descended into gazing at the sonder of those who passed beneath my window. At night, insomnia flickered through my veins, and tendons like golden fire made me want to scream and burn. I knew – or, at least, at that time, and only ever at that time – it felt real, like some heinous double of the original magnetism that made me a witness to strange things, that I could perceive some kind of hum that reverberated all over the city and kept me awake. I thought I was going insane. I bought sleeping pills, but they did nothing to help – I may as well have drank coffee. During the day, my mind only functioned with a similarly strange, heaving buzz, as if my brain had plugged in a back-up generator – something Funnel Man presumably had. Night would come again and I would lie in an empty bed; eyes closed, yet feeling them peel themselves open again. Anxiety became a melodrama, prone to fits of energy that scrawled paranoid messages, barely containing the screams in my head from overlapping into my mouth. I would moan fiercely that I was alone and that I could not join everyone else in losing consciousness. Just to lose consciousness, to sleep, is the grace of madness. I sat up all night and cursed like Satan.

***

It was only when Paul Thompson died that I finally slept. Funnel Man had been absent and no one had really noticed. The last that had been heard of him was that he was ill or had had an accident, no one could fully remember. Stories got mixed and the stories all but soaked up his existence. On the day of the funeral, I could not stop smiling (and I tried my best to disguise it) because I felt I had witnessed another clue again – just when I thought it had fallen from me altogether. I went to a large DIY store and bought several tins of paint in conflicting colours, along with a handful of brushes. I had no idea of the design, but I was going to create a public mural to Funnel Man in just the way that Thompson could never have comprehended. Yet, it would also be everything I had ever wanted to scream in his face fashioned into one pristine display. I decided to paint it on the building of the university department where he used to work before they threw him out.

I worked on it in the small hours on a wall public enough to get noticed, but one that had no security cameras pointed in its direction. It had taken me a couple of reconnaissance missions to locate the right wall. Among the cameras, I remembered the secret police: where were they now? Luckily, I am a white man: they would not think of coming for me unless I did something obvious and overt. Each time I stalked around the environs, I tried a subtle look around to see if anyone was there. No one was. On the night I started to paint, I wore all black to remain as incognito as possible. It was not long into painting, however, that I doubled over in oppressive laughter. It was the kind of laughter that, even to me, made the hairs on the back of one's neck stand on their ends as it hollowly cracked between the buildings. What exactly I was depicting, I could not tell – some childlike drawing of a smiling Thompson lovingly touching his funnel, which spread to be touching all those around him, who were smiling, too – all of which had loose resemblances to the staff members of the faculty. I drew myself, in such a way that it made it ambiguous as to whether I was being merely touched or penetrated by the funnel. The overall effect of the completed mural reminded me of a psychotic drawing in ketchup and other condiments I had seen a child create once in a restaurant.

It also reminded me of a dream I had around that time, now that I was able to sleep. (Not that the insomnia disappeared altogether. Some nights it would unaccountably be there, refusing to let me drift off; after a while, I developed tactics to deal with it, allowing my mind to spin into increasingly eccentric loops until I realised that sometimes I would not be sure whether I had been dreaming all along after all.) A group of others and I were performing horrible experiments on creatures that were already in some way partially mutated, but we only made the mutations worse. This was all done underground in some great cavernous network. There were trains with carriages and we would load the failed experiments onto the trains. The trains were sent off into the dark and came back empty. Some members of the group would simply shoot the mutants. There were also massive muscular dogs and panthers, which would eat what we could not load onto the trains or shoot fast enough. One of the mutants I dreamed of was a four-foot-high chicken shaped like an egg with a head at the top, two blind unblinking eyes and one massive foot at the bottom. Then, my perspective within the dream altered so that I was one of those chickens being eaten by dogs. The perspective shifted back; I was human again. The slaughter never seemed to stop, but eventually we decided to venture outside the caves and I recognised the topography. The recognition afforded no wonder, no mystery, but stated itself as a simple fact taken for granted. I had seen the landscape last in its heyday, with cities and forests and beaches, but it had subsequently evolved into a foreign biology while retaining some familiar shapes. Perhaps there was a trace of nostalgia as I looked around, but I felt no sadness for the irrevocable changes it had undergone. Walking up deserted streets that time and nature had reclaimed, some of the group would disappear suddenly into the houses and appear in the windows, mind-dead, with advertisements. We dragged them back, but this kept on happening and it soon became a cyclical and futile endeavour. Most of the group disappeared and I left the street alone – before anyone else, myself included, was lost as well.

Turning back to the mural, I reflected on its decrepit ambiance. I hoped that in the day it would not look so eerie and, as the paint dried, it would not be so liquid and appearing to be moving autonomously to the hum of the funnel beyond death's vale. The empty cans of paint and ruined paintbrushes I left in a neat pile by the closest bin. Returning home, I piled my paint-splattered clothes into a bag and discarded them into the neighbour's bin a few doors down. The half-light just before dawn smeared its way across the sky as I nestled, still laughing to myself, for a few hours before I would have to return to the scene just to see its effects. Later, I found out there was even an article about my mural with a captioned picture of my artwork alongside a photograph of the late Paul Thompson in the local newspaper. The response of those who just walked by and only gave it a quick glance before hastily moving on disquieted me more, however: what was it about the mural that made them quicken their step?

Looking at it in the daylight, I felt an affection for my work, seeing it akin to the leaving card a primary school student would give to their favourite teacher. True, there was also something faintly disturbing to it – not least due in part to its immense size and character portrayal, and indeed to the imaginative bio-mechanical make-up of the late Thompson depicted – but people looked at it as would someone witnessing a street fight: without wishing to be seen. To my amazement, the mural stayed intact for three whole days. Then, I noticed a piece of paper tacked to it saying that while the gesture of painting a mural to the late Dr Thompson was solemnly appreciated by the faculty, it was nonetheless painted on university property without due authorisation by the heads of staff and will therefore be replaced by a plaque detailing the achievements of Dr Paul Thompson throughout his career at the university. The next day, people in overalls with a van full of thick white paint painted over the masterpiece. The job needed several coats and, for a few days after the work was started, the faint outlines of Funnel Man could still be traced. Eventually, the faint traces disappeared and a plaque was duly erected: the plaque in brief stated his name, the dates he was born and died, and that he was a former lecturer at the university.

***

The episode of the mural ushered in a new era of creativity for me. I felt inspired to paint watercolours of whatever came to mind. I would begin depicting one thing, but my amateurism led to mistakes that I rectified by trying to morph the object of my painting into something utterly different. When I became bored of watercolours, I moved on to oil paints. I tried to paint from the inspiration of another dream of mine. Paul was there.

In the dream, claws were everywhere, growing and stretching across the world. The claws were black, made of a mixture of oil, glass and iron, and were rupturing through the sky and the earth, and people were disappearing – myself and Paul assumed they were dying. For some reason, we had faced this sort of thing before and we were not too worried. A pattern would soon emerge that we could decode and then figure out how the claws could be undone. Games we knew tended to encourage the emergence of patterns, so we decided on a game of poker. This took place in a giant warehouse and, throughout the game, we explained our theory of apocalyptic patterns to nodding heads. The game sadly failed as the cards were circular, too many people joined the game and I could not distribute the cards properly. After a while, we decided that this tactic wasn't working and we went outside, a little more desperate to find the pattern because the claws were everywhere. I realised that a tall man with grey hair and a green coat – who I had seen earlier in the dream, but hadn't paid much attention to – had reappeared. I bellowed at him to get his attention. At first, the man would not listen and tried to get away while I was explaining the theory of apocalyptic patterns, so I had to restrain him, even though the man soon seemed to grow more confident by what I was saying and stayed by the side of me and Paul. He did not take much convincing; the threshold for sufficient reasoning probably changes considerably in apocalyptic scenarios. At this point, however, the claws got Paul. (All my dreams seem to have this matter-of-factness about them – where what would be an emotional climax in a film is almost glossed over entirely by my unconscious.) Paul crumpled up and became small like the size of a toddler in my arms, becoming smaller until eventually he disappeared.

I accelerated the search for patterns, but I had the inescapable feeling that Paul was irretrievably dead and it was too late. The theory of patterns had only worked while there were two of us and now that there was only one, the pattern could not fully reveal itself. By now, almost everyone had disappeared, bar the man in the green coat who was still by my side. The streets were empty, except for the claws – some of which were frozen, others still making slow cyclical movements like solar flares. Even so, I did spot some people in party outfits – dressed in 1920s art deco-style fashion – running down the cobbled streets and into the part of town where the streets got narrower and were lit with gas lamps. The man and I ran after them, past all the blank houses until we came to one that was lit from the inside with a pink glow. We went inside and found a very exclusive party, seemingly the last party in existence. We were not invited, but I managed to get past a bouncer by mumbling we were with Mrs. –'s daughter. I have no idea who that was meant to be, given she had never made an appearance nor even been mentioned previously in the dream. Regardless, we were let in. It was cramped, people were laughing and I slumped in a corner. I did not know if there was anything left that I could do – I was with the last people. Suddenly, one of the poker players from the warehouse, who had believed everything I had told him about patterns, walked towards us from the far side of the room, smashed his glass against a table in passing and buried it into my chest. He yelled in my ear, 'You fucker, you fucker with your theories and philosophy!', while I (with no remorse for life, thinking that death would be no bad thing and that it would, at least, relieve me of this absurd responsibility) yelled back at him, 'You stupid fucker! You stupid, stupid cunt!'.

My dream ended underneath the man's furious gaze. Awake, I painted the claws stretched across the sky. I painted the warehouse and the last party there ever was. Sometimes I had the urge to paint a slogan or rhetorical question around the scene. I had no training in blending colours without them appearing muddy, so I stuck to block colours like in advertisements and found it all very amusing. After a few of these, I began to paint as if

I were designing posters echoing the old Nazi design. I had no idea what I would do with these after they were finished. I feared that if I displayed them, people would acknowledge them, and I would inadvertently accelerate the fall of Weimar rather than encourage the celebration of its life. I compensated by sticking them around the flat like a private exhibition.

***

Outside, on the streets and in the coffee shops and offices, the Weimar Republic was falling still, into new and unknown abysses – abysses similar but with new strains that make things march differently now. It invaded the space I inhabited and sat down on the seats and helped itself in the cupboards. Escape, that was my only thought now. I would flee. All this witnessing meant I had seen too much and I dimly realised that when a republic falls, there are always those who are persecuted. I remembered all those notes I had taken long ago and I imagined the dark figures of officers stalking the rooms I had only just vacated in time. Would it happen? Now? In ten years' time? Something has gone horribly wrong, even though it was seen coming decades ago. So, when will it happen? When will all the prophecies of all the scientists and mad priests come to pass? And did I even want to be around when the walls fell into the ocean and the parliaments were set ablaze, when the gas ran out and only the riots kept you warm?

***

I boarded a train not knowing its destination. Across from where I sat, there was a notice. It read: *Take your seat before the train arrives.* I did not know what to make of that; it occupied my thoughts very intensely for a while, trying to make sense of it. I bought a ticket from the conductor who looked confused that I did not know where it was that I wanted to go. I just said to the final stop. Return? No, one way. Eventually, he charged me the fare. Even though I was on a fast-moving train, the sense of arrest was palpable as I sat with nothing to do. I tried to glance at my fellow travellers, but nobody ever looked up. I looked out of the window. I dimly caught my reflection and the reflection of the entire compartment superimposed onto the horizon in the window. I imagined what it would be like to paint a picture of someone looking out of a train window and staring only at the reflected interior. The reflection would, in turn, have another reflected interior in it, and on and on it would go, until the outside world would never be seen again.

***

The end of the line. I stopped running; after a while, you soon realise there is nothing except more fields and more road. It eventually ends, the road, but I will never be bothered to find out what lies at the end of it. Tar degenerates into gravel, which turns into a dirt track, which peters out into nothing at all, but a barely identifiable trail until all is lost. Just endless crop fields. Yet just before that I reckon I would recognise every single window along all the roads I have been down throughout my short life and even remember what I occasionally saw going on inside them. Turn *volte-face* and you begin to head towards the town and there you will initially encounter only single-storey buildings meshed between cheap supermarkets. Charity shops. Budget stores. Plastic roofs with scabby pigeons nesting in them. Everything is plastic, cheap, temporary. Someone here is presumably turning a profit, but all the people here appear almost senile. However, no discontent shows on their faces – perhaps due to the idea of other places elsewhere appearing fictitious.

After all, everything you could possibly need is already here, albeit in a degraded way. It is a place that is simple, it does the job, people live, although if you asked them what they did last year I doubt they would be able to tell you. All that matters is the week gone by and the prospects for tomorrow. Today is going alright. Went to the shops. 'How's you, then?' 'Same old, same old.' Roundabout. Closed pub. Hairdressers, nail bars, pizza takeaway, corporate coffee, betting den. Property services, car services, employment services. Hanging baskets decorating the town square, which has nothing in it. Everyone is dressed as if they are going to the gym. Car park, free for customers only. Have you paid and displayed? Carpets and flooring. Opticians. Barbers and bridal outfits. Funeral directors. Dentist. Reception. The church is now a community centre. Clinic. Solicitors. To Let. Sold. Town centre – all other routes. Reserved parking only. Business Park. Danger of Death – Keep Out. Find everything you need in store now. Click and collect. Interiors kitchens bathrooms. Care and nursing home. Any enquiries, please call. Thank you for travelling with us today. A thousand and one slow surrenders that make up any life. What have we crept into? What have we done? This is where the horizon spreads out flatly with nothing to show for it. I have never asked, but I can only assume the people here dream of events that have long since disappeared. Here they all are, just before the floods begin to settle, before the power stations blink and shut down, before all things melt away like clouds against the burning heat of the sun.

Further away from the centre, things are held together only by scaffolding. Corrugated iron roof. The sound of crashing metal. Rusted ventilation shafts. Another field of anonymous crops. Shipping containers, gravel, a building marked by broken windows and a warning sign in blighting yellow. Plastic garden chairs that nobody sits on. People live here, but you do not see them – only fleeting visions. Static mobile homes with lace curtains. Bins. Ad hoc red-brick constructions storing something never to be seen again. Gas pipe. Gas cannisters. Doors rusted off their hinges. Faded graffiti. Red crane. Satellite dish. Skips with nothing in them. Bricked-up windows. Over there are people doing something that cannot be seen, but they are deep in conversation about it regardless. Things taken over by the undergrowth. Broken ladders. A sign advertising a failing company. A corrugated iron wall, around 20-feet high, means nothing can be seen beyond there. Barbed wire winds its way around the top in vicious loops. Stinging nettles and weeds and brambles gather at the bottom. The ivy has grown so large in places they have become false trees. Rotting tyre. Forklift truck. Pallets. Things are seemingly only held together by endless skeletons of scaffolding. A van pulled up. Somebody got out with a box and did not know where to put it. They looked around, confused, and eventually placed it somewhere. Then, they climbed back into the van and drove off.

***

Most events in life do not take place; more encounters fail to occur than do. The world is far less interesting than it is made out to be, even if sometimes it seems that there are only ever last days. There can be no stories from over here, only obscure images and sound recordings dredged from apocryphal sources. My advice to those who still live: raise your glasses and sing one last time – you will feel all the better for it afterwards.

***

The hotel room I wanted, I was not given. Instead, I was set far lower and close to the ground than I wished and people from the streets passing by could see through my window if they craned their necks slightly. Even so, it had something of a view and I, at least, was not on the ground floor with only a wall to separate me from the car tyres and rats. I lay down with my legs crossed on the bed, still in my jacket, which rumpled uncomfortably over my shoulders. Looking outside, I felt calm and alone. Occasionally, the question of why I was here would flash through my memory and then recede into the distance – unimportant, ephemeral. I had checked in some time before and had not left the room since, not for food, nor to explore the new surroundings of a city I had never been to before. A vague thought nagged me that I should go out and at least do something, but I throttled it with my head on the pillow and said to myself that I still had plenty of time. This may, after all, be a permanent move.

As I had expected, nobody had noticed my departure. Why would they? No phone calls, no worried emails. I trained myself hard not to think of people thinking about me; it was juvenile, seeking that kind of attachment. I was annoyed at myself that even I was not immune to that secret yearning for someone to miss me, even though I had done nothing worth being missed. It was almost as if I had been let go – yet I still needed to learn how to detach oneself. I looked across towards the desk, which held a pile of notebooks and papers. I had even brought a couple of books for me to read in my grab-bag, but I could not train my eyes to follow a single line. I thought about writing with no intent; drawing or painting now seemed a ridiculous performance and thought back to my brief but lively indulgence with photography, sound and film as a manic lapse of judgement. Yet, after everything, I had still managed to retain that sharp apprehension that made me take the hotel room in the first place.

There were bad vibrations in the air: even in this new environment, they could not be dispelled. Perhaps I had not been bold enough; perhaps I should have fled the country, gone somewhere I could never be understood nor understand in turn. Even now, there was that absurd pragmatic element that anchored me to routines, made even more absurd given they should have been abolished the instant I had shuddered against the apprehension. I had run and then sat comfortably in this hotel room. My own actions made me laugh. Maybe the world was calm, at least in this corner. Maybe the wars on other continents would spread and I would be forced to join. Thought abstractly like that, it did not bother me too much. I imagined there would be a secret relief felt by many when they would be enlisted – a relief that life had been bracketed off and directions had been made clear, given from the top down. Naturally, it meant nothing to think like this. Only when faced with the genuine prospect of its reality would my thought have value. I thought about civil war in my own nation; it did not seem even a possibility. No one would know which way to march. No, life like this might go on without any major catastrophes felt to their full force, just with a gradual degradation set in as each year gets progressively worse. Longer cues at the supermarkets for food that is not there and more people joining Mushroom Ed's ranks. Violence would be sporadic and undirected. Riots, not mass movement. Perhaps I would be fine, after all; there was an attraction to that kind of chaos.

***

From the hotel window, I saw that on the opposite side of the street, there was a group of pissed kids: the boys made constant guttural noises that stood in for laughter and the girls had seemingly stopped caring about how far their skin-tight dresses rode up. One girl, paralytic, fell over in a fit of laughter. Instead of helping her up, one of the girls began playfully kicking her and another joined in. Soon, their kicks stopped being playful and, as I watched, they met with increasing force onto the girl's stomach, neck and head. The boys joined in once they had detected the slaughter of the weak. I mutely wondered whether I should intervene, but stood acutely mesmerised and watched as one of the boys also fell over mid-kick. They attacked him, too, with rage and disgust, eventually getting tired or bored as a couple of police officers walked by.

The police immediately intervened and forced them to leave (I thought that somewhat odd: shouldn't they be making arrests?), even though the group was already walking away, chatting and laughing. The bodies were still on the concrete ground, but the boy had, at least, lifted himself onto his elbows. The girl was breathing, though from what I could see it looked pained, and she was crying, cowed into a foetal position. The scene was over. The officers were leaning over the bodies and said things I couldn't hear, and I thought I should quietly close the window as if I wasn't there. Nobody had noticed me watching the entire scene.

I had just begun to pull the window to when the girl seemed to come alive and realise that there were faces peering down at her. She screamed at them to fuck off through frightened tears – aside from that, she did nothing but stayed curled up. I closed the window without saying a word. The boy was on his feet now and stumbled in the opposite direction to where the group had gone; it appeared that he was oblivious to my presence or his friend on the floor, or that the police had come. The police picked the girl up from the floor without any struggle, crossed the road again, walked off and disappeared as well. I followed them as far as my gaze would let me from the window and it occurred to me that it was as if they had arrested the girl. There was nobody else around.

But that night, I dreamt of the scene again. This time, I was outside on the street with them. It was night still and the violence continued in front of me. There was a low murmuring voice over my shoulder. It said: 'Keep your eyes on the moon.' I never saw the person who spoke to me, but I turned and saw that the moon was gargantuan, looking almost as if it was going to crash into the earth. At the moon's most northernly point, like a patch of green moss, I saw the glow of a city and I screamed.

***

From another table in the hotel bar, I listened in to a conversation: the men in their late fifties opposite me had managed to persuade one of their friends to ring his ex-wife. He was clearly reluctant, uncomfortable and agonised at his mates cajoling. It was a brief call. His friends kept smirking all the while he was on the phone.

***

Another day, lying on bed still, I unzipped my fly and toyed with myself. Erotic images of people in poses flitted around with theoretical thoughts. The playing between my fingers had something to do with boredom, the dead time being filled with myself. This habit repeated itself when life found me with nothing better to do; it was no more or less harmful than any other set of addictions, like smoking to pass the time. I made people do plenty of degrading actions they would never consent to, while I thought it all out idly without me nearing climax. I imagined the woman at the reception desk. Why her was not because I found any erotic charm to her, but because I gratuitously chose her to be my object this time – choosing her for the evil of it. By working there, she had the aura of the hotel rubbed onto her, just because it was a transitory space where people had their affairs and illicit deals. I, however, did not climax. It just hurt slightly. I folded myself away and the erotic fantasies melted. It was all too depressing.

I decided that I should probably go down to the bar and reconnect with humanity. Maybe I would even go outside. Eventually, I left the bed, went over to the desk and moved some pieces of paper around, looking at a line here and there. They contained a mix of things: notes to the things I had seen, some lines I had tried to remember from that strange manifesto I had half-written, excerpts from books I had copied out. 'My work,' I said hollowly, aloud to myself. I looked at it again and it did have some life to it – or, at least, its illusion – and it made me smile. Maybe in five years' time, there would be some ambiguous conference where people would understand these notes. For some reason, I imagined it taking place in a crypt or a deserted shopping centre. Something about shopping centres spooked yet attracted me, in the same way that supermarkets did and hotel receptions. I saw myself through the door and walls of the complex, acting out in the same ways all else did until I erupted spasmodically and thought whether such lapses of normality was what it must have been like to be Henry Miller drunk with his cock out, clutching a woman's come-stained dress. I got close to being like that at a certain time, but not anymore. I looked out of the eye in the door. There were no police. There was no one. Not even Virgil with a burning sword nor a cleaner. Footsteps pressed above me over my head. I would have liked to bug the room above. There was an amoebic life up there, someone perhaps with a car and who could drive through the night and off a cliff, or home to a family. The prospect of either/or delighted me. I went back to my notes and tried to tack together a lecture about the fall of Weimar. Some kind of celebration to its life. I stopped when I re-read the order of the disjointed notes and they were not going to draw any audiences. Thus, I should scream it from a box in the park. But I could never do that, not really. Instead, I imagined what I had written would be printed in a small distribution, maybe only a few hundred copies. Or maybe I'd have only one printed. It would have my name on the dust jacket and I would do nothing but slide my name in its alphabetical position among all the others in a library. The formality complete, I would not need to worry about harsh criticism and disbelief among those who read it. Just for myself; a little self-acknowledgement to a season of bizarre thought. To witness does not need recognition, I told myself. With that happy thought, I finally left the hotel room.

I liked the pastel colours and thought how hotels and hospitals must get their decorative art from the same outlets. I liked the half-looks I received from other guests disappearing into rooms I would never see from across the corridors. The woman at the reception desk had gone. Even with guests and staff milling about, it still felt deserted – each one shut up inside themselves as if they had a secret they were unsure had been leaked to everyone else. Nobody's eyes seemed raised to meet another's. I found myself alone at the bar, sitting for some time before anyone came up to serve me. I stared at the hollow souls around me, thinking whether I looked any different or out of place among them. I wished I could have been absurdly high. An un-sought after wave of familiarity struck me; I felt strangely at home in the desert of abandoned souls: everyone was democratically at the same level, no one could proffer judgement without a reciprocal and equally harsh judgement settled on them. People never looked at nor spoke to each other for long yet communicated without needing to make communion. I thought that I would hate it if now some over-eager employee or demanding guest would enter and spoil everything, oblivious to the tacit ethos that each object emanated. Small voices spoke, disembodied almost; I could hardly see their lips move. At this point I hardly knew where I was, as if the room contained everything and I was a mindless guest randomly snatched at the end of the universe. At last, I went through the motions to go outside, discreetly slipping through the bodies around me, all of which pretended not to notice the wake that made an event in the room before returning to the pool of themselves.

The hotel was in an industrial estate; I had not known this prior to booking the room, but felt glad of it all the same. Among the tools and equipment of labour, I could not avoid a feeling of *schadenfreude*. Thinking again, I wondered whether that feeling was misplaced: there was something therapeutically simple to building things. Perhaps I should quit my job and become a construction worker. I liked it here among the concrete and steel – why not stay? The apprehension of the collapse of the Weimar Republic may not follow me onto the scaffolding. I wandered through the building sites, the stacks of wood and iron, deserted machinery and the high barbed-wire fences that protected the warehouses and eventually found the path that led to the river. In the dark, the undulations of the water looked like oil. The path ran alongside the riverbank and I could see where at high tide the river lapped over and onto the path, threatening to drown what lay beyond it one day. On the river, I occasionally stopped to admire the houseboats. From one, a plume of woodsmoke emanated through a chimney. *A boat is the right idea*, I thought. *They are prepared for the floods; action taken.* I kept on walking, seeing no one, until I came round to where I could see my own hotel window and craned my neck to see into the black square that presumably still bore my imprint. I thought about what I must look like from the other side, and if I saw myself standing and staring like I was now, whether I would be afraid to witness the doppelganger made to replace and fit perfectly into the life I had evacuated, one that does not think like a fascist and only dimly guesses at what this version of myself thought.

I turned away and continued along the river. I thought it was beautiful how the streetlights distorted in the water's reflection. There came a bridge and I came halfway across it and stopped. I toyed with the idea of jumping into it, closing my eyes to imagine the slam of frozen water crushing my organs upon impact and being carried away numbly. It was not such a bad thought. There was even something faintly calming to it. I imagined someone creeping up behind me. Stabbed in the neck. My sight would go red as my blood leaks into my eyes and the feeling ebbs from my limbs. I saw myself being decapitated with a hunting knife. The blade was sharp enough and the hand strong enough. My body left behind and my head taken back as a prize, a tribute or proof to whoever the masters were. I smiled at my own vanity, which placed myself at the centre of the drama. Nobody wanted me dead – I had never written nor said anything worth condemnation, nor smiled at the wrong time in court, even as I rebuilt everything I had seen in all its various and failing ways.

I looked around me and I was definitely alone. A light then streamed across the sky and disappeared. It made no noise; I realised a few seconds later that the UFO was a firework that had failed to ignite and explode. In the interim, however, I had been certain that it was a missile and someone, somewhere, had finally chosen that the tension was enough and that this foreign town would glow for the last time. This is where I would meet death, under a nuclear sky: the mushroom cloud would smear away the twilight and rip away my lungs and eyes from my body. I waited for it to happen; the night remained dark. Unless it had been aimed at another city, I calculated that it would have struck by now and each second that elapsed was proving its non-existence. The time had passed. I was now living in the post-false-strike age. Another history had suddenly taken course, blowing backwards in these moments I was still alive. I had neither drowned, been stabbed or swallowed in a radioactive orgasm. It was ridiculous.

I came off the bridge like a performer after a bad act from a stage. That there was no one there to register this absurd embarrassment was worse; it was even more of a false pantomime than before. Elsewhere, Weimar fell. I kicked gravel into the waters. How long the task of witnessing would go on for, I could not tell – much of the time, I caught myself wishing that it would leave me alone. With horror, I considered that witnessing might be an infinite task, one that would take up all my days to attempt completion, but would slide between my fingers at each juncture. I wished there was a machine that would compile everything for me automatically, one that would flawlessly incorporate every new moment of witnessing to expand the vision I saw. It would be like it had a mind of its own, one that eternally comprehended as I supplied it with more fragments. It would look like a living theatre. I saw its organs from the cranes and debris around me. A house of non-stop performance and documentary; an eye on the world, which reproduced it as it was happening and showed where it was all wrong. A great play, film or some kind of moving museum, whose rooms changed in a kaleidoscope of utterances. It would somehow be everything that I guessed at when I went off to witness; a hall of mirrors to everything that pointed towards where it was going, yet at any point could strike and turn about-face into new worlds.

I quickened my pace to stay with my accelerating machine, until I faced the doorway to the hotel and smiled a childish smile as I wished that this hotel could house the gargantuan displays. Each room a gallery, a cinema, a stage, everything – an eternal hotel of extravagant imagination.

What a refuge that would be from the crumbling Weimar; a little house to hide in until the coast is clear. A little society we could have, a duck-out from those who are monstrous and want to hurt us. I thought of what I figured was an appropriate name for the establishment: The Imperial Panoramas.

***

The hours in the hotel were anonymous. Something about the wallpaper, perhaps. Or the somnambulists who wandered the corridors. I dreamt that all the photos and videos of me as a child had been gathered and made into short films and advertisements. My image had been pasted onto films already made, so it looked as if I had been acting in them, even though it was a recording that had been spliced into the film. Very strange; I had not been asked permission to use my image and I had no idea how people had got hold of all the materials – and why me specifically? I walked towards the cinema where these films were being shown as an art exhibit, but was detained by several people so that I never got to see those bizarre intrusions of privacy – even though I did in a way. My dreaming brain gave me brief and flickering images where I vaguely recognised myself.

***

I still had not left the hotel; I felt that I could not leave just yet. When I had stayed beyond the time I had booked for myself, the hotel staff and the managers looked suspiciously at me and spoke to me falteringly as if I were, in some way, untouchable or contagious. I paid for the extra few days and then they suddenly relaxed and smiled at me again. I had evidently saved myself from apostacy. Those who took my money saw that I had no attachments nor was there for any underhand business, and they left me alone seemingly imagining that I was clearly another dimensionless human being whose commitments would catch up to me eventually. As long as I was paying for those drinks I continuously drank alone, they didn't care. I knew my money was running out fast, but I couldn't muster any willpower to do anything about it. There was a serene joy knowing that oneself is sinking, yet doing nothing at all to avoid the inevitable impact. A joy in the fall; something definitive.

***

On rare occasions, I plugged headphones into my ears to channel music and sounds directly into my brain like a fast shot or hefty dose of something. Making my panorama across the unfamiliar environs, I saw it through Henryk Górecki's 'Symphony No.3'. The undulation of the music brokered a detachment from everything and each object transformed itself into an artifact. Listening to it, I tried to form the image of the forgotten prisons that people had found themselves landed in and the messages written on the walls. Things still carry on, nevertheless; they still write poetry, continuing the long, long project of distilling horror that has perennially occupied our species while vehicles drive on past. At times, my pace slowed almost to a halt, but the signs and the lights and the people pushing past me would convulse me into faster movements again.

Later, when I had returned to the hotel, I heard the symphony again. I was not playing it; it came from a radio nearby. However, there was something wrong about the piece. It did not start at its natural beginning and someone began speaking over it – I congealed into a petrified listening as I heard a bank promote their wares and security. *Something is terribly wrong here*, I thought, as if the message was saying that if all those people had only given their money to the bank, they would still be alive. Looking around, nobody else seemingly had noticed the gross error – perhaps some were, at this instant, opening accounts with that bank. I realised I would just have to accept it, like I had accepted everything else.

***

Beyond me, arrangements were clearly underway. For what, I did not know. For Jahr Null, perhaps. Fireworks ricocheted around the walls and bodies directed themselves to tasks, which I observed as if I were watching them through an aquarium. I did not bother to ask questions, but just accepted everything as it was. It followed its own internal logic and that, apparently, was good enough. With no one to speak to (every guest held themselves apart from all the other humans in the room, certain that they were apart from the scene – perhaps some even had the arrogance to believe they were above the surroundings they had lapsed into), I wrapped myself in silence. Every now and then, I would make a note of an explosion, a strange hand gesture or how the atmosphere shifted slightly when certain people entered the place. Each time, I half-expected that whoever the newcomer was that they were looking for me. They would clasp their hand on my shoulder and pull me around to look me in the face and make the arrest, but that never occurred. Each time, while also surveying the hall, newcomers would shiftily mumble something about a booking. The faces would then all turn away as they recognised another directionless individual like themselves returned into their midst with surprise and some form of disgust that no one could put their finger on. I saw myself rotting away in there and I silently hoped that there would be some opportunity, something as vague and as mad as joining a renegade circus, that would make me want to leave and be among all the others again. To be clear: I hoped not for redemption, but for relief. Perhaps that girl filming everyone at the supermarket would wander by, offer me her hand, while holding in the other the camera, and we would go off recording the workings of supermarkets together. Perhaps Virgil would ride by, hair aflame, and I would unsheathe a hunting knife and hold it out to him in salute, and my life would take the shape of playing Sancho Panza to the new Don Quixote, eking out a life between twenty-four-hour gyms and fearful tourists. Commandeer a tourist bus with a steel-pushing army, their minds warped by steroids, and ride it off a cliff to the yells of ecstasy. No one came; I was alone.

Each night, I would get drunk, starting from some anonymous point in the day and eventually, around midnight, I would stumble through the doors to escape the encroaching cabin fever and meander along the riverbank to mull over my blank thoughts of the day. Only then as I walked would The Imperial Panoramas return to me, barely seen on some bleak street like some underground bohemian palace. A small dirge might creep out from beneath the door, which would make most walk swiftly on by, but some others would stop, somehow recognising the tune, and enter. As a front, there would be a bar, but somehow concealed beyond would stand The Imperial Panoramas in all its many ways of existing.

***

I thought about The Imperial Panoramas when it reached its heyday. Somehow, I saw it being surrounded by Paris in the nineteenth century, with carriages and people in exuberant dress and masks. Everything somehow exuded a faint green light. I was disappointed with this image; it was the procession of images handed down to me without anything of myself there. The guests filled out the seats and as I looked closely, there were people there I recognised, and their dress and gestures became recognisable. The theatre in the round aged; new halls were added to make way for the galleries of odd colouration with passages breaking off infinitely with shadows and light, indecipherable shapes and people milling through them, with it being obvious that everyone knew each other intimately, echoing around the chambers with squalls and laughter. I saw the libraries made with care and love, the windows looking into courtyards dimly seen with orange light and the people there in the gardens, whispering what would never be heard again. The night was long and perhaps it would never end, and we would have to see each other always in candlelight. I smiled and wished I could cry. The Imperial Panoramas aged; the world around it got bigger and squeezed the stages and cinemas. The clientele died, replaced by new men and women with different styles of living. But they died, too, all too quickly. The Imperial Panoramas still stood, but over the decades it was held together only by a skeleton crew, doing the rounds of dusting the surfaces and reconnecting the film to the screen, hoping it would play again one last time. The wood rotted; the sign above the door wasted away and eventually became illegible. Only those who already knew where it was entered, but left soon after seeing how it was falling into ruin. But that was when I loved it the most, when the ghosts slid through the waxwork and spoke to me, and only my own bestial voice rang out in the empty halls. Here was the longest aeon of The Imperial Panoramas' life – the long dusk; the old age that far outstretched youth and middle-age. Solitude among the mothballs and ruins.

***

I imagined great statues of the human frame, ones that towered over the buildings of the old city, transfixed in gymnastic poses hailing towards a god of something that had come to be, yet nobody knew exactly what. Domes and strange towers would stick out of the earth like fungus broadcasting signals – the architecture from 2666 would be as I imagined Berlin to be were it the capital of the world. But, of course, 2666 is an impossible year – one that could never exist. Those buildings would be turned into great gambling halls and opium dens and in its shade The Imperial Panoramas would rot along with everything else, still crouched behind its earthy mask. The architecture of 2666 would never exist; The Imperial Panoramas would never exist. Instead, Teflon and Gore-Tex, the forever chemicals contained within them, would exist, along with the skeletons of the fifty billion dead chickens eaten each year by humans, which would form a crust in the land for the next intelligent life form to assume were the dominant species on earth of the time. All the ways in which people could live but do not were buried with me and my collection of everything I had witnessed. It became a subterranean cavern; I had now fully broken from the world amid my objects and fantasies. There was a peace of sorts there; a peace of memory getting lost, of the sound of water dripping from the walls. I would curl up there and relive as much as I could, everything playing around me again, and I would see from that privileged seat everything, everything and everything, over and over again. It all existed, every moment of it, splitting off again in its most wild moments to make an intoxicating garden all of its own. I saw it in the hidden breath clouded over by the things that became definitive, but were still caught up in there somehow, leading an existence that pointed to its reality. I smiled at the thought. Things could have been different, but they were not, so let us pray that alternative universes do exist and it is there that we can live out what we could have done, leaving us to ourselves here, stuck, left with the task of rioting.

I had walked far and had come to a standstill in an unfamiliar environment. I felt that I could keep on walking until my feet bled, then collapse and die and be mistaken for another homeless victim and be buried anonymously. I did not seize that opportunity, but instead turned back and The Imperial Panoramas wound itself apart in my mind with each step becoming more conscious of itself. Returning to the hotel, there was no one left. The lights were on and I heard indistinguishable noises in the back rooms. Silently, I lifted my heaving limbs up the stairs and pulled my key through the lock to open the door to my room.

Turning on the light, I saw that it was bare. There was nothing to suggest that I had ever been living there. Everything was gone: my bag, my clothes, and the vague documents and sheets and computer and everything I had written was gone. Someone must have taken it away. Used it for evidence; maybe they would take it up with me later – perhaps they had already found the notebooks I have left behind and had found me as the sole and alone conspirator. They had cleared it away silently so that nobody could ever have access. Wiped it down, disposed of it. Thinking more clearly, I soon realised that someone had come in to do the cleaning and had anonymously put it all in the bin. I silently congratulated the genius of the cleaner for their oblivious wisdom.

Now, no one will ever know. It was as if the poems of Dante had never been rediscovered or if not Dante, then some terrible double, a writer of horrific poems – poems that should never be rediscovered. I fell onto the bed face down, not bothering to undress, and dropped into a restless sleep.

***

I dreamt of a weeping child: his arms hung limp in his lap as his shoulders convulsed. The child was in despair, not merely crying, but weeping as if his life were already over – the kind of weeping that children make, then there is an earthquake. I stroked the child's back to comfort him, but the weeping only continued and my sympathy got caught in the same despair as his. I could only weep also. The scene became overtaken by a swirling blackness, blackness in all its shades swirling into electric-oil patterns to resemble arabesques or Klimt or Klee – so black that it almost became purple or orange. And it was dissolving, burning, chemically eroding into the blackness that was also a white light cut with shocks of blue. Both the black and the white were the same substance, but the white bled sharply into the black. The white light was in the shape of a woman's smile and she was smiling as if she was happy to see me.

***

The next morning, the sky burnt brilliantly. I had to shade my eyes so as not to make the pounding in my head any louder. I had no money left and could not remember whether my wallet and official documents had been thrown away with everything else I had on me. Rising slowly, I felt that everything was telling me that if I just walked through the doors, I would not be stopped. Nobody would even know that I had gone; nobody had known that I had come. Only the servers in some desert corner in America that tracked my location knew where I was. It was time to leave. And go where? This task of witnessing had to end. It was clear that it belonged to someone smarter than I, more prepared in the soul for its touch. I hoped someone out there was doing a better job than me.

I opened the door and stared down the hallway, momentarily losing myself in the ensnaring patterns of the carpet. I pulled myself back to absorb my surroundings once more. I knew it was time to leave and I savoured the feeling of being at the threshold. I looked around the room a final time, taking in all its banal corners and pressing into my mind the image of the view outside. Ripped and fluttering, a bin liner had caught on the barbed-wire fence just outside my window and was holding itself out into the wind like black sails.

Milton Keynes UK
Ingram Content Group UK Ltd.
UKHW050249280624
444818UK00006B/104